MW01232152

Otherworldly

Nick,

Thank you!

xo,

Alara lee

1

I am a sad bean, and I hope this book makes you a sad bean too!

-Allora Lee

Contents

Chapter One...7

Chapter Two...19

Chapter Three...31

Chapter Four...42

Chapter Five...53

Chapter Six...63

Interlude One..71

Chapter Seven..79

Chapter Eight..90

Chapter Nine..98

Chapter Ten...105

Chapter Eleven..113

Chapter Twelve..121

Divine Tales One...128

Chapter Thirteen..137

Chapter Fourteen...145

Chapter Fifteen..153

Chapter Sixteen...161

Chapter Seventeen...171

Chapter Eighteen...179

Epilogue One...188

Chapter One

Dawn in a New World

Rise of Autumn, Week 1, Day 8

'This one is interesting.'

'Should we take her?'

'Same stakes as usual?'

'Of course. Mera? Are you staking your usual claim?'

'Very well, I say you will not break her —no matter the outcome. My terms are one lunar year of no interference. Deal?'

'Deal.'

'Deal.'

It was a normal day. Everything went as it should. I woke from a rather vivid dream, but I still felt refreshed. Unwrapping myself from the warmth of the man next to me, I gave him a kiss on his forehead as I slipped away to take a shower and get ready for the day. Today was, by and far, going to be boring. A few operational meetings to decide on our company's trajectory, a call with another Dome to discuss a new contract with the Highlands, lunch with my least favorite coworker to discuss if she will be transferred to my division—no, she will not— and several reports needed to be pulled before end of day.

I briefly caught myself in a mirror —all sharp angles and scowls— as I made a coffee, calling out to my fiancé, "I'm out. I'll see you tonight, dinner with mom, yeah?"

A smile danced across my lips as I heard his garbled affirmative, and I took my time after locking the door to make my way downstairs. Once I was outside, I was unhurried as I walked through the Dome —watching the light reflect from the towering buildings of glass and steel, the red haze of dawn cast the world in an ethereal glow.

It was only a short walk to the office, and as I entered I felt my face harden, my voice chilled, even the steady clacking of my heels became more controlled. Every clack turned into a crack that drew attention. Coworkers who nodded heads and said good mornings, subordinates who stepped to the side as I passed, a Director who rushed to me to prep for our meetings. It was a normal day. Nothing had changed.

Yet, something *had* changed. As I settled into my office, I looked over the Dome I called home. In the short time between entering the building and sitting down, dark clouds had rolled in. Only this storm was within the Dome. I frowned. Such a thing was impossible. Then, lightning began raining down, and thunder boomed as torrential rain fell from above the city. My eyebrows rose in shock. The Dome was *protected*. This couldn't be happening.

It was a normal day.

Until it wasn't.

Until there was a sharp crack immediately outside the windows surrounding my office, and glass began raining down on me.

Until the roof followed afterward, bringing along metal pipes and wooden beams.

Until I stopped breathing.

Until darkness consumed me.

Until I opened my eyes in an unfamiliar room.

And I *remembered.*

I immediately shot up from where I was lying, swiveling my head around. I absorbed everything with a horrified look on my face. An oversized room, big enough to have a blue wooden chest, a large bed, and a mirror propped up against a wall with both a sitting and dining area. The walls were made of grey stone, decorated with stars and moons painted in pastel pinks and oranges. Gold edging embellished the empty spaces between the pictures. The high ceiling had several strands of lights crossing from one section to the other, giving off a pale light. My hands were still gripping the blanket that had been covering me before I had jumped out of the bed, the light blue cloth the only thing preventing my nails from digging into my hands. Something about the room was off. As if everything was slightly too tall.

Slowly, I brought my eyes down. I was wearing a white nightdress that fell to my knees, knees that weren't quite as far from the ground as I remembered. The ground, that must've only been a few feet from my head. My hands, with fingers shorter than I remember and nails wiped clean -a stark difference from the long, artfully painted nails I usually had. It was then that I remembered the mirror across the room from me. Snapping my head up, I locked eyes with a little girl in the mirror. Blue eyes met blue eyes, and I brought my hands up to my face. It was *different.*

My eyes... are brown. I thought to myself. Covering my eyes, I blocked out the room, taking a deep breath.

"I'm dreaming." A smile began creeping across my face, "Of course, this is a dream. I must be drea-"

[System Integrating... 2%]

"What is this? Ha..." Feeling pressure in my head, words appeared within a floating verdant green-colored box. Uncovering my face, I quickly looked around, the box remaining in the center of my field of vision no matter where I focused my eyes.

[System Integrating... 18%]

"System? What..." I paused, a sharp laugh escaping my mouth, "Like a game?"

[System Integrating... 36%]

"A dream. Yeah, a dream could have such a thing."

[System Integrating... 59%]

Pinching my arm, I felt the lingering sting, "I thought you weren't supposed to feel pain in a dream?"

[System Integrating... 70%]

"I thought letters weren't legible in dreams?" Hysteria slowly leaked into my voice, and the wavering grin finally fell from my face as I looked around the room again. The room was clearly meant for a young girl.

[System Integrating... 83%]

A young girl. *But I'm 28.* Gripping my arms, I began shaking my head back and forth, "No, no -this isn't possible. It's not-!"

[System Integrating... 98%]

I began gripping the sides of my hair in my hands, curly black hair coming again into my sight, "No! I have blonde hair. *Blonde.*"

[System Integrated]

[Congratulations! You have Awakened! System unlocked.]

[Congratulations! You've experienced an otherworldly phenomenon! Experience accumulated.]

"Otherworldly... phenomenon?" Forcing myself to release my grip, I lowered my hands to my sides, focusing everything on the box in front of me.

[Congratulations! You have experienced intense trauma threatening your mental stability and remained sane! You've learned the skill: Mental Fortitude.]

"Wha-" Before I even finished, more and more boxes started to appear below the one in my vision. As soon as I read one, the next one flipped up.

[Congratulations! You have memories of another world! You've learned the skill: Otherworldly.]

[Congratulations! You have shown arithmetic skills any Scholar would be proud of! You've learned the skill: Quick Calculations.]

[Congratulations! You have discovered knowledge forbidden by the Gods! You've learned the skill: Tight Lips.]

[Congratulations! You have been noticed by the God of Chaos, Grel! You've learned the skill: Steal Nerves.]

[Congratulations! You have been noticed by the God of Order, Brel! You've learned the skill: Sophism.]

[Congratulations! Due to being directly influenced by several Gods you have unlocked the Divinity stat! You currently have 32 Divinity.]

[Congratulations! Due to the God of Chaos, Grel, you have received an additional 25 Divinity! You currently have 57 Divinity.]

[Congratulations! Due to the God of Order, Brel, you have received an additional 25 Divinity! You currently have 82 Divinity.]

More and more, confusion settled into my mind.

"Grel? Brel? Gods? *Divinity?*" I paused, re-reading the boxes again, the meaning lost in translation.

That was when a knock brought me out of my thoughts, and the door across the room began opening. With as much speed as my small body could muster, I ran back into the bed and covered myself in the blanket. Forcing my eyes shut, I waited for whoever it was to leave.

"..."

The person took a few steps into the room, making their way to the bedside.

"..."

They were just standing there. I tried to keep my breathing slow, which was easier than when I'd been breaking down reading the boxes earlier.

"What are you doing?" The person, whose voice was distinctly young and male, sounded not quite annoyed but less than thrilled, "Eunora."

The boy paused for another moment. I could feel him crouching close to me. I could hear his breath close to my face, just on the other side of the blanket. My heart started pounding in my chest.

"Eunora!" With a start, my eyes popped open as the boy whacked me on the forehead, "You're such a faker. Hurry up, Lina has breakfast ready."

I pulled down the blanket from my eyes and took in the face of the boy in front of me, he couldn't be older than 8 or 9, but the resemblance was striking. His bright blue eyes matched mine, and his hair was cropped short, the front just long enough for a single curl to form. He was quite a cute kid.

Theo. The name popped into my head as the boy took a step back and twirled on his heel, heading out of the room.

Who is Theo?

[System Error: Memory damage suffered during integration!]

Memory damage?

[System Error: Memories attached to soul not found!]

"Wha-?"

[System Error: Solved! Memories attached to soul located!]

[System Notice: Beginning stage 1 out of [8] of memory integration! All memories from age 7 to present importing.]

As I read the notice, I felt something in my mind unlock. It felt as if I was waking up in this room all over again.

Images flooded my mind —of young boys and girls playing in a garden —a sixth child left sitting on a bench alone, of horse riding lessons with a vicious woman, of tripping over a rug that suddenly moved. Memories of a life I didn't remember. No, memories I *did* remember. As they ran through my head, the memories fell into place in my mind. Yet they were incomplete. I could tell the memories were recent and tinged with bitterness. They were not everything. But I was lost as to how I could *know* that even with the cryptic messages being sent by the 'system' —no, the [System].

There is no other way to describe the sensation but to say that suddenly I became two people at once.

I am —— ——, 28 years old, a successful businesswoman. An only child. I am Eunora Dawn, seven —no, eight years old, one of six children. I became both an adult passionately in love and a young girl dreaming of a prince to save her. I am both an educated woman and a child who has just learned to read. I am both a human of Earth and a citizen of Maeve.

And then I became one, forced together like a broken vase soldered with molten gold. I hadn't realized it before, but my old name disappeared. At that moment, the loss of my name wracked my body, and I began to shake.

Everything began falling into place around me. I knew where I was. I knew Theo was my brother, barely more than a year older than me. Hateful. Disliked. I could *remember.* I knew why Lina made breakfast. Memories of the governess teaching a young Eunora how to daintily drink tea, how to sing, how to read. It was a jumbled mess of memories. They hurt to focus on.

So instead, I took a breath. It was all I could do.

"It's okay ——. No. ——. My name *is* ——. " As I tried to pull my name out of whatever recess it was forced into, I felt my voice grow frantic as a steadily growing ache formed in the back of my head. With every attempt to say my name, the pain grew. Suddenly, it was so intense my vision was tinged in darkness.

That was when I focused and saw the [System] again. Bright even in the darkness. It took everything in me to focus and process what I was seeing.

[System Notice: The skill [Tight Lips] has been forcefully activated for the first time. Strike Cause: User attempt to utter Otherworldly name. Data currently purged. Strike Null. Grace Period in effect for: 71 Hours 02 Minutes.]

[Warning: After Grace Period expires, every third strike begins a Purge of Otherworldly Knowledge that the user attempted to or successfully shared.]

Dread settled into my stomach, and I closed my mouth. Within seconds the pain faded, and my vision was back to normal, but my hands still shook, and my legs were heavy as I sat back down on the bed.

I can't tell anyone. Not now, not ever. How am I supposed to go home? My face contorted at the thought. I covered my mouth to muffle the dawning scream. My eyesight was blurry once again, this time with thick tears that fell with abandon.

I screamed into my hands until my throat grew sore, my sobs caused my chest to ache, and my tears were unable to fall anymore. Whether it was ten minutes or an hour, I couldn't say how long I broke down for.

"If I can't tell anyone, I can't go home," I croaked in a small voice as I finally settled down. Laying back into the mattress, I stared up at the small lights strung across the ceiling. They sparkled like stars in front of a background reminiscent of the morning sky. Rich pinks, pale purples, deep blues. The room was fit for a Dawn, and the thought struck me violently.

"Eunora Dawn, who are you?" I whispered, "And why have I become you?"

Why was I brought here? Why was I taken from—. I swallowed thickly, the tears threatening to return. I forced the thoughts back. I couldn't risk his name being taken from me. I wouldn't be able to handle it.

I took a haggard breath and held it for a count of five before slowly releasing it.

Then I did it again.

And again.

And again.

Until finally, I could breathe without shaking.

I want to be alone. I don't want anyone to disturb me. Not until I'm ready.

So, I rose from the bed and made my way to the ornate stone doors that, based on a flicker of a memory, would lead to an opulent hallway filled with paintings of this world. Of the family I've been forced to join. Of the land I now stand on. As I clicked the lock in place, I felt my stomach turn.

More flashes of memory filled my mind.

The Count and Countess Dawn. Eunora's mother and father. A distant couple, continually away from the manor. Never present when Eunora needed or wanted them.

Raphael Dawn, 15. Eunora's eldest brother. The first son and heir apparent to the family. In her memories, he is a liar. He pretends in front of staff and family alike, but never once has he sought out his younger sister. Currently attends a swordsmanship academy in the capital, only returning once a season for their break.

Evelyn Dawn, 13. Eunora's eldest sister. The first daughter and a mage in training. She is brilliant with a spell —just as Raphael is skilled with his sword. She is calculating and cruel. Currently studying at one of the local Mage Towers. Resides at the manor.

Theo Dawn, 10. The second son. A scholar. He never forgets something he's read. Though he has not yet been allowed to choose a permanent path, he currently has several high-level tutors come to the manor. He believes Eunora is useless. Dumb and weak and without magic.

Eunora was the fourth child, freshly turned 8. She was not a swordsman or a mage or a scholar. She could read and write and learn, but a prodigy she has never been. She was quiet and withdrawn, polite but never outgoing. She was lonely.

Leonard and Leah Dawn, twins, 6 years old. The third son and daughter. Sweet children that have had the love of the eldest three Dawns for as long as Eunora can remember. The ease with which they received love causes a pang to resound in my chest.

A remnant of a feeling not my own. A *Eunora* feeling.

As the day passes and I refuse to acknowledge the [System] notifications that have appeared in the back of my mind, I continue to simply stare —out the window overlooking the labyrinthine garden below, up at the ceiling's twinkling lights, even at the dawn themed wall decorations. I simply stare and ignore. And briefly, I wonder if anyone will fetch me for a meal or a party or even a simple congratulations.

Today is, after all, Eunora's eighth lunar birthday. The day she Awakens. The day the Sun Gods allow her to choose her birthright boon. Four solar years. A Divine day.

Of the Dawns, not one came by to see her —*me,* I was forced to remind myself.

There was only a light knock from a maid asking me to open the door. When I refused to respond, she simply walked away.

As the second Sun hung low over the horizon, I tucked myself into bed and ignored the growl of hunger. I was not yet ready to face the eyes of the manor. Not even for food.

Chapter Two

Path of Order

Rise of Autumn, Week 2, Day 1

I woke up slowly. There was no confusion in my mind about where I awoke or what it meant. My eyes were sore, and my throat was hoarse, after all, but I was still here. Still in Maeve. Still in this unfamiliar yet familiar room. Who had been crying last night? Was it _____ mourning those _____ left behind for this world? Or was it Eunora, whose family only acknowledged her when she was within eyesight? I couldn't tell who was hurting or if they were even separate at all. The adult I was tells me that not all families are perfect, but the child I am feels pain wracking through her. The child I am tells me that death is small, but the adult I had been screams that I could never understand her pain. Something was lost from both sides of my soul. And now, I simply feel weary and confused about who I am meant to be.

The dreams from the night before were no simple thing. They were intense and felt akin to a nightmare. They were memories. They were memories from last year, memories from Rise, the first month of spring. The lunar year was halfway through, and Eunora had just turned seven. The Dawn family was having a tea party, though the seats for the Count and Countess sat empty. The memory focused on the shadows that seemed to edge Eunora's vision, her desire to scream and cry and beg her siblings to see her. To hear her. To show she existed. None of them did. Theo and Raphael sparred with sticks. Eve mesmerized Leonard and Leah with a [Skill] —the one she received as a Boon on her Awakening. The five of them gave a cursory hello and then left the seats next to Eunora empty. The remainder of Rise was a mix of the same. Except for once, when Eunora went to her reading lessons with Lina and, upon returning to her room, found the door sealed. Eve had bound it with magic and forced her to sleep in the hall —stating those without talent should lay like a dog on the carpet. The Dawns had no need for someone who did not know her place. Eunora cried herself to sleep until, upon waking in the early morning hours, she found the spell had worn off. Then she curled into her bed and refused to leave her room until after dinner the following day. No one came then, either.

Now, I was looking outside the far window to watch as the red sun had risen while the yellow sun still lingered on the horizon, painting the world in its crimson hues. It was a beautiful sight that forced a sense of dread into my gut, so I pulled my blanket over my head and tried to go back to sleep. It was too early for such tragically peaceful sights.

Instincts and memories pushed themselves to the forefront of my mind before I could cocoon myself back into bed. I felt a sense of excitement at the [System] and the dreams about what my status would look like. No—Eunora's dreams. I blinked. Ah, right. Taking a deep breath I thought to myself: *[Status]*.

[Status Summary]

[Name: Eunora Dawn]

[Race: Human]

[Age: 8]

[Unallocated Stat Points: 0]

[Vitality: 7 Endurance: 4]

[Strength: 6 Dexterity: 8]

[Perception: 9 Magic: 4]

[Luck: 45 Divinity: 82]

[0th Tier Class: Child of the Gods, Max Level]

[Boon: Not Selected]

[1st Tier Class: Not Selected, 0 Level]

[Skills:

0th Tier:

1st Tier: Quick Calculation Lv. 1

2nd Tier: Otherworldly Lv. 1, Mental Fortitude Lv. 1

Untiered: Tight Lips Lv. 1, Steal Nerves Lv. 1, Sophism Lv. 1

[Congratulations! You have opened your Status Summary for the first time! You have unlocked a Boon from the System. You've acquired the skill: Inspect.]

[System Notice: As a first time System User, Inspect will be automatically activated for the following items: Vitality, Endurance, Strength, Dexterity, Perception, Magic, Luck, and Divinity.]

[Vitality: Often known as one's lifeblood, the Gods decreed "Be Well. Live Long. Thrive." upon bestowing the value to mortals. The main effects of Vitality are enhanced general health, enhanced recovery, and reduced aging speed past adolescence.]

[Endurance: Often known as one's physical will, the Gods decreed "Continue to Charge. Stand Firm. Endure." upon bestowing the value to mortals. The main effects of Endurance are enhanced stamina, enhanced stamina regeneration, and the increased chance to withstand catastrophic injuries.]

[Strength: Often known as one's capacity for force, the Gods decreed "Enforce. Destroy. Dominate." upon bestowing the value to mortals. The main effects of Strength are enhanced battle acuity and optimized muscle growth.]

[Dexterity: Often known as one's ability to maneuver, the Gods decreed "Be Nimble. Be Graceful. Avoid All." upon bestowing the value to mortals. The main effects of Dexterity include enhanced agility, enhanced fine motor control, and enhanced speed.]

[Perception: Often known as one's ability to absorb information, the Gods decreed "See All. Hear All. Understand all." upon bestowing the value to mortals. The main effects of Perception include enhanced attention to detail, enhanced reaction speed, and enhanced mental processing.]

[Magic: The Gods decreed "Bear Your Will, Show Your Intent. Bend Nature As You Please." upon bestowing the value to mortals. Unlike the five physical attributes, Magic is built off the soul. The main effects of Magic include mana control and mana sight.]

[Luck: The Gods decreed "Good Luck." upon bestowing the value to mortals. Unlike the five physical attributes, Luck is built off the soul. It is believed the effects of Luck include enhanced probability sense and higher-order deduction skills.]

[Divinity: The Gods decreed "Rend the Earth. Steam the Seas. Contort the Very World." upon bestowing the value to mortals. Unlike the five physical attributes, Divinity is built off the soul. The effects of Divinity depend on the Gods whose will the user embodies, as well as the Will and Intent of the user.]

[Notice: Due to your Divinity level, you are capable of viewing three messages that await you. Would you like to accept them?]

I took a moment to process the sheer volume of information before taking a breath.

"Yes."

[Acceptance recognized. Messages being pulled for display.]

[Message 1]

[Welcome, Otherworlder! You have awoken on the planet of Gargantua as a noble child within the Kingdom of Maeve. As a precautionary measure, the Gods who brought you here bestowed both boons and restrictions. Use them as best you can. The Gods hope to see both your successes and your failures.

Congratulations! All abilities from your previous world have carried forward! The [System] will integrate them as your experience from your past life is applied.

May your Eternal Star burn Bright.]

[Message 2]

[Otherworlder,

I have taken parts of your past to help you integrate into this world. Have no fear, they will be returned upon completion of your purpose.

It is recommended that you integrate the memories of your body and continue on her path.

Lord of Order,

Brel]

[Message 3]

[Otherworlder,

Cast off your chains and forge your own path. Whatever Chaos you bring, I will be watching —so make it good.

Lord of Chaos,

Grel]

I frowned as I read the messages. From Gods. And one that sounded suspiciously similar to the [System] itself. I chewed on the inside of my cheek, anxiety snaking through my chest.

Gods brought me here. And they want very different things.

I let out a steadying breath. This was a new problem, something I hadn't even considered possible until the stream of skills the day before. Brel and Grel. Order and Chaos. Two sides of a single coin. And neither seem benevolent. They forced me here, after all.

A purpose. I hunched forward, holding my head in my hands, the meaning sinking in. *If I want my old name then I need to fulfill a purpose.*

Brel says stay the path —Grel says forge my own.

I would have thought I would be crying again at the overwhelming thought. But instead, it was as if I was broken. No feelings came. Not indignation at being ripped from my perfectly fine life, not grief at losing everyone I loved, not excitement for gods or swords or sorcery. Exhaustion filled me, and I laid back down into the bed, another notification filling my mind with a deep green screen.

[System Notice: As a first time System User, Inspect will be automatically activated for all newly acquired skills from the past 24 hours.]

I tried to care about them, to think through what the system had given me, but as the wall of blurbs filled my vision I was unable to summon the excitement of the past Eunora. I settled for simply straightening up.

[Otherworldly: After being ripped from your previous plane, your presence here is a rare occurrence — though not unheard of. As an Otherworlder blessed with Divinity, your presence will not go unnoticed. The first to be served, the last to be reprimanded, and the one chosen for destined encounters. Through this Skill, your Aura is passively expanded. With additional Mana infusion, this skill can define your presence further. Range increases per level. Definition increases per level.]

What does it mean to be defined? I thought to myself, as I internally cringed. A social skill is the opposite of what I wanted. Not that I wanted anything at all. In fact, had the [System] not already pulled the rest of the [Skills] I might have simply stared out from the window —taking in the view of the dual suns as they rose above the horizon.

Instead, I read through the rest. Trying not to sigh at the Divine related [Skills].

[Mental Fortitude: You have had your mind shaken to its very core. By being exposed to such traumatic mental attacks for a lengthy period, you gained the ability to partially nullify mental instability passively. In times of immense distress, this skill is capable of enacting treatment and coping mechanisms in order to restore stability. Total effect is increased per level. Evolved treatment and coping mechanisms learned with each level.]

[Quick Calculation: Your base knowledge of arithmetic has allowed you to surpass a majority of the world. When you are solving anything related to a mathematics formula, you will be exponentially faster. Speed is increased per level. Complexity of formulas able to solve is increased per level.]

[Tight Lips: You have uncovered knowledge forbidden by the Gods of this world. Should you try to share this knowledge, the Gods will become aware of your attempts to undermine them. Whenever you are questioned about forbidden knowledge, a signal will be sent to your mind as a warning. Should the warning be ignored and information still be attempted to be shared, a strike will be recorded. After every third strike there will begin a purge of otherworldly knowledge that you attempted to or successfully shared and a relevant God or Goddess will review the purged information to determine validity. Increased purge precision per level. Increased pain per level. This is a restriction skill.]

[Steal Nerves: You have attracted the attention of the God of Chaos, Grel. For his entertainment, Grel has gifted you with the ability to thrive on chaos. Whenever you are in an unsatisfactory situation, and you are plagued with anxiety and self-doubt, you may

siphon confidence from the party you are up against.
Grel often uses this when someone confronts him over
his many, many pranks. Total effectiveness is
increased per level. This Skill cannot be used on
inanimate objects. This Skill is dependent on your
Divinity attribute being above 0.]

Instinct told me this was a dangerous skill. So dangerous I
decided to simply ignore it.

It most definitely did not matter that, for some reason,
Grel had made the Skill name a pun. Or that it did not
specify what siphoning confidence did to the subject. I
pointedly did not linger on the unbidden thought that
mind magic is rare and dangerous —and *hated.*

[Sophism: You have attracted the attention of the God
of Order, Brel. In order to help guide you to the
proper path, Brel has gifted you the ability to see
Paths to Order and Chaos. Whenever you are making
a decision, your perception of time will slow, but your
processing speed will not. The skill will help your
rationalization of events and will occasionally give you
direction on which is the Path of Order and which is
the Path of Chaos. This skill is directly affected by
your Perception stat. One second can be slowed by a
factor of 5 for every 1 Perception. The effectiveness is
increased per level.]

I knew this Skill was a trap. It screamed it from the
rooftop. Choose the Path of Order enough, and I will do
as Brel wanted —live as the ghost of a Eunora long gone.
Choose the Path of Chaos enough, and who knows what
could happen. The [System] had not said Grel was an Evil
God —or that Brel was Good— but Chaos does not strike
comfort in one's heart. This was already proving to be an
exercise in futility —fighting the will of the Gods.
Perhaps, if I only pick the middling options each time

then they will leave me alone. The [System] had already implicitly confirmed I would not be going home after all.

Phrases such as *previous life* and *new world* were not hopeful terms.

I dismissed the boxes and fell back onto the bed. All I wanted was for sleep to reclaim me, but it did no such thing.

Instead, the numbness that had sunk into me began to fester into something darker. A resentment of my circumstances.

In *elsewhere*, I had been subjected to tragedies —no one goes through life without a major misfortune or three— but this was incomparable. While those had never been so devastating, in no small part due to the support from friends and family, I had still never felt *defeated* by a tragedy. Not like this.

Ripped from my life by the whims of two gods. One who wanted me to submit and continue on like a ghost, and one who wanted me to take the path of most resistance, to change the very world I now found myself in.

[System Notice: Class selection unlocked. Due to memory integration, Class selection is recommended to be withheld until Stage 3 is finished in approximately 35 days 15 hours 08 minutes and 23 seconds.]

As I stared past the green notice and focused on the dainty lights that decorated the ceiling, I couldn't help the chill that settled into my bones.

I didn't want to make a decision about classes. Not when I *knew* about it without ever remembering *learning*. Instinct is a horrible feeling when it comes from a dead soul within me.

I spent the day alternating between staring at the ceiling, listless, and staring out at the garden from the window, irritated. It wasn't until the sky started to darken that a knock on the door resounded.

I stood up and glanced at the mirror propped up. I was in the same white nightgown with pale purple embroidery that reached my knees, my skin was fresh in the way children never had to worry about acne, and my hair was wild. The black curls shot in every direction. The knock came again.

This time, the door shook but did not open. I had, after all, locked it yesterday.

"My Lady, I have brought dinner."

I decided to open the door, but before I could say anything, the woman had strode past me —her nose wrinkled when she glanced my way— and set down a silver tray with two covered plates, an empty tea cup, and a teapot.

I felt an ache deep inside of me as if Eunora was weeping. And I felt rage bubble under my skin. Rage at these feelings I couldn't control. That were plaguing me against my will. These childish whims and thoughts and reactions.

I watched the woman whose name I *knew* but did not know —and thus refused to think about— as she deftly set up my meal. Within a minute, silver was laid out, and the covers were removed from the plates to reveal a salad made with aquamarine leaves —*waterlily* screamed in my head— and a dish of some potato-like substance with red meat. Gingerly, the woman poured a cup of tea —*rose tea, my favorite.* I shuddered.

"Leave."

It was all that would leave my mouth as I stared at the dinner in grim horror. *Favorite.* I hated it. The very thought that my tastes had changed to meet this body's likes and dislikes. I wanted to scream.

The woman was gone within moments, the purple and white fabric of her maid's uniform rustling with the speed.

I sat, staring at the food, for several minutes.

People and plants and animals I had never heard of granting me their names unbidden. Simply popping into existence. Meanwhile, my own name was lost to me. I was not *hungry* —not in the way I should have been. It had been two days without food. I should be starved. But my mouth was dry, and though I could feel the ache of hunger, I did not want to eat. The thought of consuming anything filled me with waves of nausea.

But I was not the type to waste away. Not like this. Not without understanding.

So, I ate.

I hated every bite.

Chapter Three

Path of Chaos

Rise of Autumn, Week 2, Day 2

The dreams were harder to process on the second night when I knew what they were. It would have almost been better if her family had hit her. If they cared enough to hate her. To torment her. But it was small tricks with little thought; it was forgetting her existence. It was that I could *feel* her heart break with every slight. It was as if it were my own.

I suppose, in a way, it *was* my own.

These memories of indifference and apathy began to eat at me. And still, I refused to leave the room.

Rise of Autumn, Week 2, Day 5

I felt the power of [Otherworldly] coursing through my veins when I awoke, my very being keyed into my surroundings. It felt as though even a fly would be unable to pass me by. Just as quickly, the surge of the skill faded.

A full season filled my memories. Five months of Spring. Five months of Eve sneering and mocking, of Raphael avoiding me, of Theo's petty tricks, of seeing Count and Countess Dawn monthly. Cold stares and unfeeling words. I was sure without [Mental Fortitude], I would be feral at the very thought of the Dawns.

The same maid had dropped off dinner each night as I holed up in my rooms, but no more. Yet still, I was not hungry –not in the way someone *alive* would be hungry. The memories showed me how little I had done. For a whole season, Eunora had barely spoken, hovering in the background like a specter. Haunting her own family home.

But with the completion of a season came a [Skill] fit for the way the child had spent the Spring of her seventh year.

[Congratulations! Due to integrating the memory of your feats pre-Awakening, you have received the Skill: [Silent as a Shadow]!]

I released a sigh as I looked out over the glowing horizon, "[Inspect]."

[Silent as a Shadow: You are noticed yet ignored. You lurk, yet no one cares. Like a shadow, your presence is taken as fact. This skill allows you to blend in, to hide in plain sight. So long as you do not draw undue attention to yourself, it is harder to be found suspicious. This skill requires mana to maintain. Ability to mute your aura increased per level. Decreased relative perception per level. Duration limited. Cooldown applies.]

"I hate this System," I groaned and rolled out of bed, making my way to the windowsill. To my left was a washroom that I had only used as needed, never actually finding the will to bathe; meanwhile, to my right was the sitting area and a door leading to a walk-in closet filled to the brim with lavender and blue-violet clothes. Until Awakening, those are the only colors permitted to children of House Dawn. Now Awakened, I am allowed red violet and pastel pink as well. In several years, pastel orange and crimson will be allowed, then light yellows and blues. Never green. Green is not of House Dawn.

Green had been my favorite color in *elsewhere*.

The irony of my System being green was not lost on me.

I tucked my legs underneath me as I sat on the window sill, examining the garden below. Maybe one day, I would leave this room and walk through it.

That day is not today.

Rise of Autumn, Week 3, Day 2

Another surge of feeling occurred as I awoke. This time, it felt as if I was running [Quick Calculation] on a never-ending string of formulas. Only, the answer never revealed itself.

[Congratulations! Stage 1 of memory integration complete! All memories from Age 7 successfully imported! You have gained the Skill: Weave of Darkness.]

Sometime in the past, Eunora had picked up a hobby of knitting; it seems she did have something she was rather adept at, after all. The memories of her alone in her room often included her knitting or crocheting small projects. Early on, her skills were mediocre, but as the year progressed, so too did her dedication. It explained the basket of soft knit animals she had tucked below her bed. One of which was a deep violet bunny with silver eyes.

[System Notice: Beginning stage 2 out of [8] of memory integration! All memories from age 6 to 7 importing.]

"[Inspect]."

[Weave of Darkness: Through dedicated practice of your craft, you have been rewarded with the ability to turn shadow into wool. This skill requires mana to maintain. Increased darkness affinity per level. Increased durability per level. Decreased cost per level.]

I knew, somewhere fueled by [Quick Calculation], that my mana was only enough for a fist-sized knit object or a napkin. And even that was once per day. I wondered, briefly, if I even liked knitting. In *elsewhere,* I had never been one for such things. I was the type to chat and drink and experience. This was the type of hobby that was calm, meant to soothe the quaking of one's soul.

My eyes landed on the edge of the basket holding all of the knit objects and crafting supplies, and out of curiosity I spoke.

"[Sophism]"

My vision shifted, doubling every object and causing my stomach to lurch. One layer was cast in a red light, while the other was cast in a white light. Instinctively, I could feel that the dense white light was *Order* and the dense red light was *Chaos.*

I focused on the pile of knitting supplies, willing the skill to show me what would happen if I tried to pick up the knitting needles. I choked on a snort as the two layers settled in rings around the basket. Of course, the first time would be useless. Both layers merged into an orb of shining pink light.

A phrase popped into my head, a shade of a memory: *The order of chaos.*

Then I went to the basket and removed the knitting needles. Their wooden form glowed in the same pink light -Order and Chaos in one. Both defying and obeying the Gods.

After a moment, I put them back and tucked myself onto the windowsill once more. Letting my eyes stare unfocused over the garden.

Maybe another time.

Rise of Autumn, Week 4, Day 4

It was odd going backwards into memory. And enlightening. More context arrived, but not much. More specifics of the kingdom –Queendom, I suppose. Eunora is a noble, the daughter of a Count of the Queendom of Maeve, in the Central Corridor of Opalle, the continent of peaks. The family is old –older than I had consciously thought but not older than I had *known*.

[Congratulations! Stage 2 of memory integration complete! All memories from Age 6 successfully imported!]

[System Notice: Beginning stage 3 out of [8] of memory integration! All memories from age 5 to 6 importing.]

I opened my eyes slowly. The room was still gray with low light. I was filthy.

It had been weeks since I last took care of myself. I hadn't bathed nor changed nor ate more than a single meal. It was too much. My hair was matted into a ball, and even the maid no longer entered the room to drop off dinner; she simply knocked and left it outside the door.

It was time. Even if I felt too empty to move, too grief-stricken, too dead. I rose and made my way to the washroom attached to my bedroom.

Heating the tub was a slow process, but it allowed me to take in the brunt of my reflection and the harsh reality I had put myself through. No longer was Eunora soft. Half a meal each day was not sustainable, it appeared. I ran my hand over the ribs that were just below the surface.

Fine, I thought to myself, *I will eat more, but I won't go to the dining room. Those people have nothing to do with me.*

As the runes lining the tub began to glow a dull grey, steam billowed from the edge of the water.

The magic of this world was amazing. Had I been anyone else, I would have been in awe. But I came from a world of magic; this world was no better than where I had been. That thought renewed the sting of being forced into this body once more, and a childish cry began to swim to the surface of my mind.

I shut it down before it came out and stepped into the hot water. I felt the burn immediately, the feeling of being seared stirring something within me, but I continued settling into the tub until I was fully submerged. I leaned my head back so that the matted mess of black could soak.

Stretching my body, I soaked in the water for ages allowing pain to replace the emptiness inside of me. As the runes lining the tub began to fade, the heat slowly dissipated. At the first sign of a chill, I took a bottle off the edge of the tub and began massaging the oil into my hair. I began at the tips and painstakingly began working through the knots that had overcome my head.

By the time I was done and had washed out all remnants of oil from my scalp, I had decided I would braid my hair to avoid this in the future.

When I stepped back into my bedroom with a new nightgown covering me and my hair pulled back into a thick braid, I smelled of lilacs. My eyes had trouble clinging to anything too closely. I lingered on the knitting supplies, but it felt as if it would be too much for me to find out if this body would control my likes and dislikes.

This time, when the maid left dinner, I ate every bite. I found I actually liked it.

Rule of Autumn, Week 1, Day 6

Rise, Rule, Peak, Break, Fall, Autumn, Rise, Rule, Peak, Break, Fall, Winter, Rise, Rule, Peak, Break, Fall, Spring, Rise, Rule, Peak, Break, Fall, Summer, Rise, Rule, Peak, Break, Fall, Autumn. The memories flooded me in a never-ending pattern; a month's worth of memories every night, each more solitary than the last. A Lunar Year — two seasons, five months per season. Every night comes a whole month. Revel becomes a Blue Moon. A Solar Year —all four seasons. The dual suns dance through the sky, circling each other as they circle the world. I hate that I know these ways of time. I hate that I have lived through it.

I hate it all.

This world can burn.

This family can fall.

I want to leave it all behind.

I no longer care whether I continue on, but I cannot get myself to stop trying to live.

[Congratulations! Stage 3 of memory integration complete! All memories from Age 5 successfully imported!]

[System Notice: Beginning stage 4 out of [8] of memory integration! All memories from age 4 to 5 importing.]

[System Notice: It is recommended the New User selects the Sun Gods' Boon and a First Tier Class. Would you like to perform the selection of your Boon?]

"No."

Rule of Autumn, Week 2, Day 3

Another season passes by in my mind's eye.

I know the names of the Gods. Dozens upon dozens.

I know the names of nobles. Dozens upon dozens.

I know fables Eunora heard as little more than a toddler. I know facts and fauna and flora. I know too much.

And yet it is somehow not enough.

A month has passed. A month of mentally rotting.

It leads to an unwelcome notification.

[Congratulations! Mental Fortitude has reached Level 2!]

I bathed twice more in a single week —that is something.

Rule of Autumn, Week 2, Day 8

[Congratulations! Stage 4 of memory integration complete! All memories from Age 4 successfully imported!]

[System Notice: Beginning stage 5 out of [8] of memory integration! All memories from age 3 to 4 importing.]

[System Notice: It is recommended that the New User selects the Sun Gods' Boon and a First Tier Class.

Would you like to perform the selection of your Boon?]

I took a breath, rereading the prompt.

Maybe—

No. I want to leave this world. My suffering is not worth a minor boon.

"No."

Rule of Autumn, Week 3, Day 7

The anguish of leaving behind a life half-forgotten fills me.

With it comes another System message.

[Congratulations! Mental Fortitude has reached Level 3!]

Perhaps I needed it more, or my mental state was more shaken than before. Whatever it was, I found the energy to open the window and air out my room.

Rule of Autumn, Week 4, Day 2

[Congratulations! Stage 5 of memory integration complete! All memories from Age 3 successfully imported!]

[System Notice: Beginning stage 6 out of [8] of memory integration! All memories from age 2 to 3 importing.]

[System Notice: It is recommended the New User selects the Sun Gods' Boon and a First Tier Class. Would you like to perform the selection of your Boon?]

I let the message hang above me, my eyes still bleary from sleep.

This time when I spoke, my voice was solid.

"No."

Instead, I picked up the knitting needles and decided that maybe Eunora was right.

Something to soothe me would be nice. Something repetitive and creative.

Knitting would do.

"[Weave of Darkness]"

My fingers wove deftly as if I had been learning for a year.

The skill itself produced two types of wool, pitch-black yarn that would occasionally give off wisps of shadow that faded into the ether and a translucent yarn that would reflect light back in a wave of iridescence. I cast on with a knot that I *knew* and now had *learned*.

The first row was me using a single knitting needle and my thumb, stitching the same way over and over until I reached just under three inches of length. [Quick Calculation] told me I could make several small coasters if I cut down the size. So, I did.

The second row was when the monotony began. I lost myself in the motion of the two needles and the yarn. Slide the empty needle under the first cast, pull to the right, wrap between the two needles —back to front, pull down the yarn, bring down the needle to catch the yarn, tuck the needle under the loop, use the needle to slide the stitch over to the opposite needle, begin again.

Slide, pull, wrap, pull, catch, tuck, slide, pull, wrap, pull, catch, tuck, slide, pull, wrap, pull, catch, tuck, slide, pull, wrap, pull, catch, tuck, slide —over and over and over.

Despite the ease with which the stitches came, I worked slowly, focusing on each step and creating a new memory. One of *me* —not one stolen from *her*. I spent hours that day knitting one of the small coasters with [Weave of Darkness].

[Congratulations! Due to your skill and dedication, you have learned the Skill: Weaving!]

The moon, Revel, was hanging on the horizon when the notification came.

"If I was going to get a weaving Skill, why did it come after a yarn Skill?" I mused, with a small twitch of my lips that quickly faded as my voice hardened into a command, "**[Inspect]**."

[Weaving: You have practiced the age-old art of creation using yarn and materials. By dedicating time and passion to the craft you will be granted the ability to Weave like artists of old. Increased Dexterity while weaving. Increased Skill while weaving.]

[Congratulations! Inspect has reached Level 2!]

Chapter Four

Gods of Many Things

Peak of Autumn, Week 3, Day 8

[Congratulations! Stage 8 of memory integration complete! All memories from Age 0 successfully imported!]

[System Notice: All stages of memory integration complete. Welcome to Gargantua!]

[System Notice: It is recommended the New User selects the Sun Gods' Boon and a First Tier Class. Would you like to perform the selection of your Boon?]

Half a season, nearly three months. I let my defeat wash through me as I stared at the ceiling.

"Fine. Yes." *It has been long enough. Let's at least select the Boon.*

[Congratulations on your Awakening! As a celebration of your Awakening, please pick the God whose Boon you wish to select:]

[Scylla]

[Morloch]

[Druigr]

[Qwail]

Scylla, Goddess of Prophecy and Gambling.

Morloch, God of Sacrifice and Improvement.

Druigr, God of the Second Sun.

Qwail, Goddess of Livestock and Familiars.

My memory filled in the gaps, and I felt the pointlessness overcome me once again.

Of course, ever more Gods meddling. At least this is out of some sense of benevolence.

I thought of what the tutor had said, memories coming easier than ever.

"The Gods, in their unending wisdom, knew Mortals would struggle. They knew a single solar year could make or break a generation. Thus," she had paused, letting the tension build, "They decreed that, for every Solar Year, they would elect a Patron. Hence why, upon Awakening at eight lunar years, there are four minor boons to choose from —one for each year the child has lived through. They range from a single attribute point to a lesser cantrip. The Dawns, when there is such an option, choose a deity tied directly to one of the Suns. You will be expected to do the same."

I felt my lip curl into a sadistic smile as I looked at the four options in front of me.

A Dawn would choose Druigr. A farmer or mage would choose Qwail. A Hero would choose Scylla.

"Morloch," I hissed.

Morloch, of Sacrifice and Improvement, is a God of Darkness. A God in opposition to the Sun. He is known to rule a domain that resembles a labyrinthine cave system. A realm without light. He is his own Sun. He has to be — to provide for those who worship him. Much like the color of my System, with its verdant green light, this too will set me apart from the chains the other Gods have seen fit to shackle me with.

[Congratulations! You have selected Morloch's Boon! You have gained the Boon [Morloch's Blessing]! You have received +3 to Magic!]

As I closed my eyes, my senses were overrun with the feeling of insects crawling under my skin. Of my veins opening wider. Of a sense of *wrongness.* It took every ounce of self-discipline not to drag my nails across my skin and try to dig out the sensation. I grit my teeth as power roiled through my blood. And then I let out a sharp breath as relief, sweet as honey, flooded my body. It was like a gentle rain on a hot summer day. Or the first snow in late autumn. It was a soft breeze in spring. The crunch of leaves underfoot. It was magic. And as it settled, I was reminded of *elsewhere.* As if anything could stop me from thinking of the only place I have ever called home —in this life or the last.

Only instead of the bitterness and rage and depression that had consumed me these past months I felt the peace of a pleasant memory. So rare in this world, I hung onto it with everything I had.

The memory was still clear – it had not been ripped from me by Brel.

The memory of the first time I wielded Magic in *elsewhere.* Under the Dome, where I was safe, I hadn't needed it much —but I had *wanted* it. And it was beautiful. My very soul had resonated with Darkness. I had been so good at it. It responded to me as if it was an extension of my very being.

I felt tears prick at my eyes.

Magic here was more convoluted. It required study, spirits, and contracts. It required Skills and Stats. It was why I could no longer call to that part of me that I had longed for. In *elsewhere*, magic was light and airy and filled small roles in the world. But it was beautiful. Here it is everywhere, used for everything. From the mana-fueled lights to the runes engraved on the tub —but it is *ugly*. Even without mana sight, I can feel the way it is shoved through circuitry not meant to caress the mana. Magic is meant to be delicate and skillful and intricate. It is also meant to be freely used —not limited by the fools who built this System.

The only saving grace is that the two Skills from Eunora's memory seemed to take into account my own past as well as hers.

[Silent as a Shadow] and [Weave of Darkness]. They were an amalgamation of our souls —*my* souls. I bit my cheek. It gets harder every day to maintain the separation between Eunora and *me*. Every day I call her me more often. I think of this body as mine —it is growing difficult to deny such a thing.

Especially after witnessing eight years of her life. After feeling every emotion that wracked through her. After knowing her hurt and having to push it aside.

Peak of Autumn, Week 4, Day 3

It was mid-morning when a knock resounded in my rooms. Harsh and too loud. There was too much force for it to be the usual maid —not to mention it was much too early.

I was in one of the dozens of white nightgowns I had, and my hair was woven in two thick braids. I had bathed the day before. All things considered, it was not the worst time for someone to decide to see me.

I slid off the windowsill, placing the purple bunny with silver eyes that Eunora had painstakingly stitched together gently down on the bed.

It had become something of a reminder of Her. Of who I both was and was not. Of who I could no longer be.

Whoever was knocking did so again, only with more force. I debated briefly if I should open the door at all. But something new hit me –a small *want* from who I was. Who I had been, *she* wanted me to open it. So, it only took me another handful of seconds to unlock the door and pull it open. I didn't flinch when I saw who it was, but it was a near thing. I maintained a blank expression.

"Well?" Said the boy —no, young man, at the door. Raphael Dawn. With his neatly groomed curls that reached just past his ears and his bright blue eyes –and the same frown that I see in the mirror. Whatever he is doing here is bound to be annoying and probably hurtful.

"Well, what?"

"Aren't you going to step aside?" He gestured behind me, and I briefly glanced back before peering around him in turn. He was alone. Eve and Theo were nowhere in sight.

It must be Raphael's mid-season break. I regretted giving in to *her* desires already. I should have known no good would come of it.

"No." I went to close the door, but something flashed across Raphael's face, and he snapped his hand out and caught it before the door moved more than an inch.

"That's not how this works, Eunora." His voice was rough, in the throes of deepening. I let out a huff and stepped back, letting go of the door.

What was the point of fighting him? I would just lose. I didn't even have a Class. Though that was a fault all my own.

Rather than head to the sitting area, I went straight for the window sill. The window frame was still open from when I was letting the breeze bring in fresh air and the smell of dry leaves from the garden. I picked up the bunny and sat down where it had been.

Raphael had followed me in, but he looked as if he would rather have been anywhere else.

I stared at him, waiting for him to speak. Eunora would have begged him to talk, to say whatever he wanted, to spend time with her. But I had no such desire. In fact, I couldn't remember a single time Raphael searched her out like this. It was all chance meetings and forced proximity.

He seemed to be waiting for my previous desire for his affection to make itself known. That made my dislike for him grow.

Seconds ticked by as we sat in silence —well, Raphael was still standing as there were no seats by the window.

"Out with it," he huffed.

I dug my nails into the bunny I was clutching, "You'll have to be more specific."

"Your Class. What is it? I know you've just had your birthday."

I reeled back. "Just had?"

"Yes, yes," He waved off the question, "Last week or whenever. Is it a Common Class? At the *very* least tell me you qualify as a noble?"

Last week. My stomach churned. Last week. *Eunora.*

"Out." I felt the wool compressing within my hands, the soft yarn roughly rubbing my palm. My voice was cold, chilled, *furious.*

"What?" Now Raphael was the one who reeled back, "No, I-"

"Get out," Despite the knot in my stomach, the words were strong, solid. "Out and don't return."

My eyes met his once again, and I stood, "Get out."

"Who do you think you are?" He hissed, recovering and stepping towards me. I didn't cower.

I have never been the type of person to be bullied silently. It was one thing to be neglected passively, as a matter of course, but this was different. This was in my face. And it was making me rage.

"Young Lord Raphael Dawn. Get out of my room. You have no right to question me about *my Class."*

And it was true. Had this been a normal family, perhaps it would be shared. But Class specifics for nobles are held by the head of the house. And Raphael was not Countess Dawn. The Countess hadn't even asked.

"What is the matter with you?" He took another step towards me, just a pace away, as he looked down his nose at me, he continued to hiss, "You have never called me that-"

"What? Your title?" It's true, in Eunora's mind, she had only ever thought of him as Raph. She so desperately wanted them all to love her, she wouldn't call her siblings anything but their nicknames. A harsh laugh escaped me, and I turned back to the window, "Do you even care?"

48

Whatever Raphael was going to say died in the silence between us. And it was only moments later that I heard him stomping out of the room. A resounding slam came from the door as he left.

I brought Eunora's knit bunny to my face, an odd comfort radiating from the stuffed animal. A *childish* comfort. It helped to quell the disgust and anger inside of me just enough for me to feel the edges of numbness creeping back in. My eyes were drawn to the basket beneath the bed, whereas before it was a singular basket full of crochet and knit items of purples and pinks and the occasional blue, the basket has been joined with another – this one an effort of over a week's worth of work to knit a basket large enough with [Weave of Darkness]. Each day I would weave until my mana ran out, infusing shadow into every stitch. Now, it is as if the black basket truly is the shadow of the other. Tucked neatly within is a single set of black coasters, five fist-sized shadowed chicks, an iridescent napkin, and another miniature bunny with a black body and shining eyes. Nearly a month's worth of work.

Knitting had been something to do. And along with it came the feeling of home —of shadow and darkness, the same as in *elsewhere.*

I took a deep breath.

If Raphael had come looking for me to measure my Class' worth, then soon enough, someone sent by the Count and Countess will come.

"Three months," I whispered, "Eunora, it took them three months. Can't we let them go?"

The pain radiating from my chest was the only answer I received.

At least when I slept, I no longer had to see their faces in my dreams. It was bliss.

Three months since this body left the room. Three months since this child called on a maid for anything other than dinner. Three months since anyone tried to care for her.

Out of a desire for contact, or anger at being alone, or any other number of reasons, I rose and went to the door. To the side, by the handle, was a brass hook holding an ornate golden bell. The bell was small, no larger than a golf ball, but every inch was engraved with darkened runes. They swirled and intertwined, looping around each other just to merge into a single, intricate symbol. The lines formed two stylized suns rising over the horizon. The symbol of the Dawns.

I took the bell into my hand, holding it out away from me.

Eunora rang it often —if she wanted anything. She rang it for tea and snacks. She rang it for more yarn. She rang it for books. She rang it for meals. The point is, she rang it.

I bit my cheek, deciding if this was what was next. If this was what I needed. Inside, I still wanted to be alone. To fester inside myself. To survive on the bare minimum.

I rang the bell and hung it back up, shifting nervously in front of the door. Waiting. The ringing had been quiet, so soft that without magic there was no way the sound could have reached anyone but myself. However, the runes began to give off a golden glow, and I could feel the wave of mana that was sent out. I knew it was carrying itself elsewhere, allowing whoever was listening for it to know that I had rung the bell at all.

The waiting caused a knot to form in my stomach, and I couldn't stop my hands from fidgeting with the purple bunny —which I decided must be named. Immediately.

Perhaps that was another symptom of my agitation. I was suddenly enraged at Eunora as well —she had neglected a creation of her own as she had been neglected. Immediately, I cringed at the thought.

"That's a bit of a stretch," I sighed to myself, "I think I might be panicking, bunny. I've spent three months alone, what if that's what I should keep doing?"

I pulled the stuffed animal close to me, and stood waiting for a few minutes —until a gentle knock echoed from the outside of the door.

I took a deep breath and counted down.

3...

2...

1...

"Good morning, my Lady," came the soft voice of the maid as I pulled the door open and stared at her, "How can I be of service?"

My grip on the bunny loosened just enough for my muscles to begin to relax. She was not the same maid from before —which, really, made quite a bit of sense when you took into account it was still mid-morning, and that maid usually came at night. Still, she looked rather similar, with her blue hair tucked back in the same style.

"I would like breakfast," Unlike earlier, when I had venom lacing my words with Raphael, now my voice was small, timid even.

Whatever this anxiety was reminded me too much of Eunora's disposition. I hated it. It felt as if it was not my own. Yet another chain to bear.

The maid tilted her head in acknowledgment and gave a shallow curtsy, "Yes, my Lady. I will return shortly."

To the maid's credit, she did well in hiding her surprise. Her smile didn't drop –just stiffen– and her eyes only widened a hair. Even with all of that, she still kept a gentle, kind tone. Something had stirred in me after she left. I remembered her from the dreams. I liked her. *Maria*, my mind reminded me, *Her name is Maria. And she has always been kind.*

As I sat curled up on the sofa, I looked back on the morning –on the past several months too.

While I wouldn't say I was handling being reborn *well*, I would say that enough time had passed that I had at least accepted the reality of it. The reality that I was stuck here, with no way home, born to a family I'd rather disown, chained to two Gods for their entertainment. Another cold reality is I could just die. It probably wouldn't send me home, but at least I wouldn't be here. I immediately struck that thought –I wasn't the type to succumb to that type of fantasy, and I didn't particularly relish the thought of being actually dead, despite feeling dead inside. That meant I had to live here. And living here meant using the System. And using the System meant choosing a Class.

[System Notice: It is recommended the New User selects a First Tier Class. Would you like to perform the selection of your Class? Once started, this process cannot be interrupted.]

I stared at the verdant green prompt.

"Yes."

Chapter Five

Divine Irritants

Peak of Autumn, Week 4, Day 3

[System Notice: Now beginning Class Selection!
Analyzing current experience and affinities! NOTE: A
maximum of eight First Tier Classes will be processed
for your selection based on these attributes.]

[Congratulations! You have spent 8 years as a citizen
of Maeve! New Classes unlocked!]

[Congratulations! You were born a Noble in Maeve!
New Classes unlocked!]

[Congratulations! You have an elemental affinity! New
Classes unlocked!]

[Congratulations! You have two souls! New Classes
unlocked!]

[Congratulations! You have learned many things! New
Classes unlocked!]

[Congratulations! You have been blessed by the Gods!
New Classes unlocked!]

[Please acknowledge completion of Analysis!]

"Okay," I said with a slight nod of my head, and I was
flooded with a wall of text. Eight options arose.

[Citizen of Maeve (common)]

[You are a beloved citizen of Maeve! As such, the
Queen of Maeve has placed you under her protection.
As a citizen of Maeve, you are free to explore all paths
to the future. May your life be blessed and your

fortune found. Unlocked by being born in Maeve.
Unlocked by living in Maeve. Unlocked by having
parents who are citizens of Maeve. This provides you
with +1 to Strength, +1 to Dexterity, +1 to Endurance,
+1 to Vitality, +1 to Perception, and +1 to Magic, per
level.]

[Acolyte of Chaos (uncommon)]

[You have been touched by a God. By accepting the
truth of the God Grel, Lord of Chaos, you will be
granted the title of Acolyte. Through your worship
and devotion, Grel will speak to you and allow you to
enact his will on to the world. Unlocked by being god
touched. Unlocked by receiving a skill from Grel, Lord
of Chaos. Unlocked by practicing religion. This
provides you with +2 to Vitality, +2 to Dexterity, +4 to
Magic, and +4 to Divinity, per level.]

[Acolyte of Order (uncommon)]

[You have been touched by a God. By accepting the
truth of the God Brel, Overseer of Order, you will be
granted the title of Acolyte. Through your worship
and devotion, Brel will speak to you and allow you to
enact his will on to the world. Unlocked by being god
touched. Unlocked by receiving a skill from Brel,
Overseer of Order. Unlocked by practicing religion.
This provides you with +2 to Vitality, +2 to Perception,
+4 to Magic, and +4 to Divinity, per level.]

[Student of the World (rare)]

[You are a child who loves to learn and you have been
exceedingly great at it. For a child, you have more
than a lifetime's worth of knowledge. You seek to
learn and consume all that you can, without regard for
if it should be known at all. Unlocked by knowing

arithmetic. Unlocked by knowing biology. Unlocked by knowing physics. Unlocked by being literate. Unlocked by possessing restricted knowledge. This provides you with +1 to Strength, +1 to Dexterity, +2 to Endurance, +4 to Vitality, +4 to Magic, and +12 to Perception, per level.]

[Young Lady of Darkness (rare)]

[You are a being of shadow and darkness. Your very soul agrees with that. Through your struggle, you found solace in true Darkness. A Young Lady of Darkness is both graceful and lethal. A weapon with her magic as well as her mind. A Young Lady of Darkness has the potential to rule high society from the Shadows, or become the Shadow of high society. Unlocked by being a citizen of Maeve. Unlocked by being a Noble. Unlocked by having an inherent affinity to Darkness. Unlocked by having the Mental Fortitude Skill. This provides you with +2 to Strength, +2 to Endurance, +4 to Vitality, +4 to Dexterity, +4 to Magic, and +8 to Perception, per level.]

[Young Lady of Dichotomy (rare)]

[You are a being of multitudes. Going beyond the common expression 'two-faced', you possess two conflicting personalities. A Lady of Dichotomy is able to put her best face forward at all times, and is able to pull the appropriate personality forward without any trouble. Such a Lady is able to maintain her two persona's independently of each other. Unlocked by remembering your past life. Unlocked by having an alter ego. Unlocked by having a fragmented mind. Unlocked by possessing the skill Mental Fortitude. Unlocked by being a noble. This provides you with +2 to Strength, +2 to Dexterity, +2 to Endurance, +2 to

Luck, +4 to Vitality, +6 to Perception, and +6 to Magic, per level.]

[Devourer of the Forbidden Fruit (epic)]

[Within this world, the will of the Gods is law. Despite this, you have obtained knowledge forbidden in this world. Researching such things draws the eyes of many -both divine and otherwise. Those who obtain forbidden knowledge have two paths available to them, either continue to collect knowledge that cannot be shared or to defy the will of the Gods. A Devourer of the Forbidden Fruit must prepare themselves to fight the Gods above and below. Unlocked by possessing forbidden knowledge. Unlocked by being not of this world. Unlocked by possessing the Tight Lips skill. Unlocked by being noticed by the Gods. This provides you with -6 Divinity, +4 Magic, +6 Perception, +6 Luck, +6 Endurance, +8 Strength, +8 Dexterity, +8 Vitality, and +8 Unallocated Stats, per level.]

[Acolyte of Chaotic Law (legendary)]

[The Gods Brel and Grel have shown their interest in you. Grel desires you to sew Chaos throughout the realm, to shake the very land you stand on. However, Brel desires you to protect the Order of the world, to maintain the stability this world has found. As with all things, Chaos and Order must maintain a delicate balance. You, who possesses two wills, represents that balance. You are to be the arbiter between the Gods Brel and Grel, allowing them to have a direct impact on the world around you. Unlocked by being God touched. Unlocked by receiving a skill from Grel. Unlocked by receiving a skill from Brel. Unlocked by having an alter ego. Unlocked by being not of this world. This provides +6 Unallocated Stats, +6 Luck,

+18 Perception, +18 Magic, +24 Vitality, and +24 Divinity, per level.]

"Absolutely *not,*" I hissed as I read through the four Divine related Classes.

Even I knew they were chains –Classes define a person's soul, to tie that to a God is to irrevocably change oneself.

[Acolytes] serve their Gods, that's how they gain experience and level. Meanwhile, [Devourer of the Forbidden Fruit] screams of a death sentence. No matter the stats that they grant, I knew I could never take them.

I also couldn't take [Young Lady of Dichotomy]. I would sooner rot than allow another to rule me. 'Two souls' is horrendous to think about, let alone give one rule over my body. It also is unsettling to think about being a body snatcher, the very thought causing me to shudder.

Not to mention striking the Common Class. In fact, I immediately rejected the scholar Class as well –I did well in classes in the Dome, but I had no desire to make that my life. Instinct was telling me there was a better option.

[Young Lady of Darkness]

I took a deep breath and let the world fade away. In my old world, shadow had been my natural affinity –it allowed me to see in the dark and shade my face. Shadow let me do party tricks and also protect myself. A blade of darkness is just as sharp as a metal blade. It was my soul, my comfort, my passion.

For the first time in months, a genuine smile crept up my face, and I whispered, "[Young Lady of Darkness]."

[System Notice: Please confirm your Class selection of 'Young Lady of Darkness', a Tier 1 - Rare Class.]

"Yes." I gave a sharp nod.

And then my vision went white as a slew of notifications slammed into my head, one after the other. It took me a minute before my eyes would focus on the verdant green words of the System.

[System Notice: Class Confirmed!]

[Congratulations! You have obtained the class 'Young Lady of Darkness', a Tier 1 - Rare Class!]

[Congratulations! You have leveled up Young Lady of Darkness!]

[Congratulations! You have obtained the Class Skill: Manipulation - Shadows]

[Congratulations! You have obtained the Class Skill: Conjuration - Shadows]

[Accumulated experience is being applied!]

[Congratulations! You have leveled up Young Lady of Darkness!]

[Congratulations! You have leveled up Young Lady of Darkness!]

...

[Congratulations! You have leveled up Young Lady of Darkness!]

[Congratulations! You have obtained the Class Skill: Shadow Animation!]

[Congratulations! You have leveled up Young Lady of Darkness!]

[Congratulations! You have leveled up Young Lady of Darkness!]

I had to take a moment and count the notices. Fifteen notices. Twelve levels and three Skills. I had received the initial class Skills and then the Level 10 Skill.

"This is too much…" My voice broke as a thought occurred to me.

Twelve levels meant twelve levels of stats.

"[Status]." I whispered, my throat thick with dread.

[Status Summary]

[Name: Eunora Dawn]

[Race: Human]

[Age: 8]

[Unallocated Stat Points: 0]

[Vitality: 55 Endurance: 28]

[Strength: 30 Dexterity: 56]

[Perception: 105 Magic: 55]

[Luck: 45 Divinity: 82]

[0th Tier Class: Child of the Gods, Level Max]

[Boon: Morloch's Blessing]

[1st Tier Class: Young Lady of Darkness, Level 12/20]

[Skills:

0th Tier: Inspect Lv. 2, Weaving Lv. 4

1st Tier: Quick Calculation Lv. 2, Silent as a Shadow Lv.1, Weave of Darkness Lv. 4

2nd Tier: Otherworldly Lv. 1, Mental Fortitude Lv. 3, Shadow Conjuration Lv. 1, Shadow Manipulation Lv. 1

3rd Tier: Shadow Animation Lv. 1

Untiered: Tight Lips Lv. 1, Steal Nerves Lv. 1, Sophism Lv. 1]

"Oh, this is bad. This is very, very *not good.*" I muttered as I ran my hands over my face —and promptly pushed myself over the edge of the sofa toward the ground. Which then allowed me to use my higher Dexterity to catch myself —too well, and I flung my body *back* towards the sofa. Which *then* led to my gripping the fabric with all my Strength and piercing the cushion with my nails. But I *had* stopped falling.

[System Notice: Warning! A large amount of experience was applied! The System advises taking a meditative state as soon as possible. It is estimated that your body will acclimate to the new attributes in: 11 Hours 59 Minutes 49 Seconds]

As I took in the clarity of the letters, their meaning struck me. And the barrage of feelings hit me as well.

Not only could I feel my muscles tighten, but it was as if my hair grew out in an instant -causing me to have to gasp and take in a bracing breath. Quickly, I released my grip on the knit bunny to prevent any damage and leaned into the sofa to steady myself. *That was so not supposed to happen.* Looking around, suddenly, everything got more distinct. The ridges in the stone wall, the shades of pinks, oranges, and yellows that were painted on the wall, and the tiny spider hiding in the very tallest corner of the room. Even the design on the rug looked more defined. It was too much. I had to squeeze my eyes shut to stop the incoming headache caused by the information overload.

I took deep breaths as I continued to press my face into the soft fabric of the sofa. In. Hold. Out. Hold. In. Hold. Out... It was all I could do to measure my breathing as I forcibly extended my fingers —to stop myself from clenching the fabric of the sofa again and causing further damage. The seconds inched by. The only way I had of telling time was the angle of the light that flowed in through my bedroom window. An eternity later, but really no more than an hour, there was a knock at my door.

That would be breakfast.

It took me several tries to control the muscles in my face before I was able to croak out, "Come in!"

In fact, I wasn't sure I was able to say it at all —until I heard a high-pitched yelp from behind me and the sound of metal wheels speedily rolling in my direction.

"My Lady," Maria exclaimed as she gently placed her hand on my shoulder and began attempting to guide me to turn around, "Keep breathing. I'm going to position you better. You will be all right, my Lady. I am here."

I attempted to help and flexed my arm —only to fling myself too far and land on Maria's chest. I groaned while Maria tutted at me.

"No, my Lady, simply relax your body —it will take you time to adjust. I am going to lift you up and set you down upright so you can try and eat. Your body will need the energy."

In fact, I was already beginning to feel hunger pains strike me —a new sensation since Awakening. As Maria carefully began to prop me up with her arms, I couldn't help but wonder how she knew it was System adjustments that were making me like this. Then again, Raphael *had* come in demanding my Class this morning. Perhaps the whole estate thought my birthday was only days ago. No one who knew the actual day would even fathom that I had waited weeks —let alone *months*, to select a Class. It simply was not done.

As Maria slid back, she pulled over the cart she had brought with her. With great care, she began separating out soft foods —eggs and oatmeal— from foods I would have to chew —fruits and a biscuit. Turning back to me, she began feeding me the soft foods.

"It should only take about half a day, my Lady —please do not chew. You could bite through your cheek if your Vitality isn't high enough compared to your Strength."

I found dark amusement in the fact that the only compassion Eunora was shown was from this maid. *Who else would take care of me if not someone who was paid to do so?*

As she fed me, I stared out towards the window —taking in the sight of the yellow sun hovering toward the top of the window's view. Unlike the sun that shone through the Dome, this one was far smaller —half the size of Sol at least. Meanwhile, the red sun hidden behind the top of the window was easily a quarter larger.

Anything to not think about how I was being fed like a toddler.

Chapter Six

Forced Exploration

Peak of Autumn, Week 4, Day 3

Maria stayed for a while, adjusting my body until I could be trusted to inch slowly by myself. Until the afternoon came, and she had to go. She helped me into the bed and wished me luck.

And then I was alone again. This time with ten hours left to meditate.

Well. Time would pass whether I meditated or slept, I thought. So I attempted to do just that.

Sleep never came. Not after ten minutes or two hours or even at the five-hour mark. And it was *boring*. It dawned on me, later, that being *bored* was a feeling I hadn't truly felt since arriving. But at the time, I simply thought that even though I could have used the time to plan my future or plot against my siblings, those things were useless in the *now*. So instead, I thought of ways to use my skills.

They were all I had that were *mine,* after all. Everything else belonged to the Dawns. There wasn't a piece of copper that I could lawfully claim.

[Silent as a Shadow: You are noticed, yet ignored. You lurk, yet no one cares. Like a shadow, your presence is taken as fact. This skill allows you to blend in plain sight. So long as you do not draw undue attention to yourself, it is harder to be found suspicious. This skill requires mana to maintain. Ability to mute your aura increased per level. Decreased relative perception per level. Duration limited. Cooldown applies.]

This seemed mostly a foil to [Otherworldly] if I was honest. In moments where I needed to hide from the eyes of others, to be of this world, I could mute my aura and stifle the presence [Otherworldly] gave me. In the frustration and coldness that often overwhelms me in this new world, there is something warm in this Skill. As if it was Eunora who gifted it to me rather than the System. As if she knew her chains and wanted to help unburden me, if only for a moment.

If I leave my rooms, this is the Skill I will have active. [Quick Calculation] told me with my new well of magic, I would have plenty of fuel to dedicate to it. I have yet to actually use it, but at Level 1, I felt its limits within me. Though—

"[Inspect]"

[Silent as a Shadow: 1st Tier Skill. Duration of 5 minutes. Cooldown of 2 hours. Current level of [1] out of [40].]

Without another thought, I decided to pull up [Inspect] for the first time since receiving the skill all those months ago.

[Inspect: Through accessing your Status for the first time, you have been granted the universal skill Inspect. Based on your Perception, knowledge, and Skills, you can examine both physical and metaphysical objects and receive data relating to the item in question. Increased information displayed per level.]

"[Inspect]"

[Inspect: 0th Tier Skill. Immediate activation. No cooldown. Current information display: detailed personal status, public information of sapients at or

below your level, basic name for known items. Current level [2] out of [20].]

Unbidden, a memory of a memory surfaced.

"Inspect is the great equalizer, at a high enough tier, it can penetrate the mask that individuals put around themselves. But until the third tier, there is hardly a chance to see more than an individual's class category. Noble, mage, warrior, ranger, cleric, the basics. Unless, of course, they set their status to public —but outside of time-limited commands, it's a rare person who would invite such trouble."

I recoiled at the memory of Lina's tutoring and, fortunately, was free of being near anything easily destroyed —as my hand swatted roughly down into my mattress. After deciding [Inspect] is predictably useful and likely tedious to level, I decided the first step would be continuing to use it on the rest of my active Skills.

[Weave of Darkness: Through dedicated practice of your craft, you have been rewarded with the ability to turn shadow into wool. This skill requires mana to maintain. Increased darkness affinity per level. Increased durability per level. Decreased cost per level.]

[Weave of Darkness: 1st Tier Skill. Continuous activation. No cooldown. Current length able to produce on a full mana pool: 770 yards. Current maximum tensile strength: 572. Current Weave color options: A Shadowless Night, A Shadowless Day. Current level [4] out of [40].]

In truth, the strength rating meant nothing to me. I had heard the phrase in passing, but whether it was an impressive grade or not was beyond me. However, I took a sharp breath when I realized the exponential growth of my mana pool. Before, with regeneration, I could do 100 yards in a *day*. Now I could produce seven times that immediately. That's enough to make a dozen knit animals. Several scarves. A sweater —for a toddler, but still. [Weaving] filled me with low-level ideas as I stared at the verdant green screen hovering in my eyesight.

I stared at the system prompt, attempting to dissect it before it occurred to me that the Weave of Darkness I currently made was either a black so deep it was void or so bright it was iridescent. This implied there were other shades of the Weave I could use. If I—

Another wave of power rolled through my body, shaking my thoughts. Strength surged through my muscles as more details came into focus, and a new layer of the world formed before my very eyes —it was too much. I had to re-focus and move on in order to maintain a semi-meditative state.

[Steal Nerves: You have attracted the attention of the God of Chaos, Grel. For his entertainment, Grel has gifted you with the ability to thrive on chaos. Whenever you are in an unsatisfactory situation and you are plagued with anxiety and self-doubt, you may siphon confidence from the party you are up against. Grel often uses this when someone confronts him over his many, many pranks. Total effectiveness is increased per level. This Skill cannot be used on inanimate objects. This Skill is dependent on your Divinity attribute being above 0.]

[Steal Nerves: REDACTED TIER. REDACTED ACTIVATION. REDACTED LIMITATIONS. Current level [1] out of [REDACTED].]

What a divine pain in my ass.

Without a thought, I chewed on my lip —only for it to split at my strength and begin oozing hot blood. The taste of copper filled my mouth. The moment I released the pressure, I could feel the wound stitching itself back together with my new Vitality. It *itched.*

I had to bite back the irritation as another prompt flicked up.

[System Notice: Warning! A large amount of experience was applied! The System advises taking a meditative state as soon as possible. It is estimated that your body will acclimate to the new attributes in: 2 Hours 53 Minutes 45 Seconds]

So close, yet so far. I wanted to scream. Instead, I let myself imagine a world of darkness. The element that so often soothed me in my past life. The very thing that now helped keep me grounded.

I focused on the Shadow skills.

[Shadow Conjuration: As a Young Lady of Darkness, you will become a master of the unseen. Whether you wield the darkness offensively, defensively, or passively is dependent on your will. With this Skill, you will be able to summon a hardy Shadow that can become corporeal. Total effectiveness is dependent on your Perception, Magic, and Divinity stats. Additional effects unlocked upon level up.]

[Shadow Conjuration: 2nd Tier Skill. Continuous activation. No cooldown. Current volume of Shadow able to be summoned: 3 CY. This Skill requires mana to maintain. Current level [1] out of [60].]

Inside me, I felt emotion stir. Never again would I be alone without darkness. Without the comfort of shadow. Without the ability to act. The Skill itself only allowed me to conjure shadows —not control or shape them. But the knowledge that the brightest day couldn't stop me from wielding Shadow was a soft comfort in the cold reality of this world.

Three cubic yards. That is my height more than twice over. A space of solace in the dark.

Immediately I flicked up the other half of the equation.

[Shadow Manipulation: As a Young Lady of Darkness, the world of the Nightstalker shall be yours to command. Whether you animate the shadows to do your bidding, wrap yourself in the comfort only darkness can bring, or simply wish to obscure yourself -this Skill will allow you to manipulate Shadows according to your will. Total effectiveness is dependent on your Perception, Magic, and Divinity stats. Additional effects unlocked upon level up.]

[Shadow Manipulation: 2nd Tier Skill. Continuous activation. No cooldown. Current volume of Shadow able to be manipulated: 3 CY. This Skill requires mana to maintain. Current level [1] out of [60].]

I felt something in me start to stitch back together.

Darkness. *My* darkness.

I closed my eyes. Darkness and Shadow are not the same, but, in this moment, they are everything. They are two parts of a whole. *No*, something inside of me whispered, *they are two parts of a larger whole.* The dark is of the Abyss. It is of the Void. The dark is Shadow and Darkness, yes. But it is *more.*

And the Skills were only Level 1, but all of them were impacted by 3 of my ability scores. The Divinity score most important of all. I was reminded of what [Inspect] had shown when it first activated: *The Gods decreed, "Rend the Earth. Steam the Seas. Contort the Very World."*

Become Divine. It was the purpose of the ability score. It had to be. I felt the weight of [Sophism] and [Steal Nerves] on my Status. Skills granted by the Divine. Divine intervention that brought me here. An ability score of 82 Divinity.

My stomach rolled, and I pushed onward to my last Skill.

[Shadow Animation: As a Young Lady of Darkness, you have summoned the unseen and commanded the world of the stalker. Now the unseen will use your soul to fuel a creation of your own shadow. Through your strength of will your shadows will begin to act of their own accord in line with your commands. No two shadow animations will be exactly the same. Additional animations unlocked upon level up. Duration increased upon level up. Cooldown decreased upon level up. Command comprehension increased upon level up.]

[Shadow Animation: 3rd Tier Skill. Immediate activation. Duration of 10 minutes. Cooldown of 10 minutes. Current animation options: Wisp, Infusion. Current level of command comprehension: simple. Current number of commands able to be issued: 1. Current number of animations on a single summon: 1. Current level [1] out of [80].]

Infusion?

[Animation Option 2: Infusion. Create a Shadow and infuse it into an existing construct of Shadow. Limited to Darkness and Shadow created by your own hand.]

I flicked my eyes down toward the end of the bed, thinking about the knit bunny I had gripped so intently before. The one made of [Weave of Darkness]. Made of *me*.

I could bring it alive. I waited a moment before— *Maybe.*

The ice of mana flooded my veins involuntarily, and I gasped. My body was still alternating between the heat of my enhanced body and the ice of my new magical prowess. At eight, my body and soul would be stronger than most young adults. A single level of a Tier 1 Rare class granted four times the stats of a Common and twice as much as an Uncommon. At Level 5, that was the equivalent of a maxed Level 20 Common and a Level 10 Uncommon. At Level 10, that was a max Level 20 Uncommon. And I was Level 12. On pure stats alone I outclassed most below the age of thirty. At three months Awakened, most children were Level 1 —or 2 if they were ambitious.

All children start with Common class options, but 1 out of 100 are offered Uncommon. And 1 out of 10,000 are offered Rare.

As my body settled once more, I felt resignation weigh me down. And right as I started to drift to sleep, I gently brushed a hair out of my face.

[System Notice: Congratulations! A large amount of experience was successfully applied! It is estimated your body has substantially acclimated to the increased attributes.]

Interlude One

Hands of Dawn

Peak of Autumn, Week 4, Day 3

With hair of a soft blue and eyes of molten amber, Maria was a beauty. She was young and sweet and, for all intents and purposes, *average.* Her sheets were the average amount of soft, her tea moderately hot, and her sweets just extravagant enough for a county maid. Again, Maria appeared to be an average maid. She was mild-mannered and kind to children. She spoke only when called upon. She was just as a maid should be. But Maria was *not* all she appeared to be.

As she slipped out of the room of the newest Awakened member of House Dawn, she hastened her steps.

Her [Inspect] had shown a simple [Noble] tag, but Eunora Dawn was suffering stat sickness. In the extreme. After not leaving her room. Not that such a thing is *odd* for a child of the Dawn —they have been notorious in ages past for their peculiarities. Even the youngest twins, Leah and Leonard, have times when they spend days in their rooms. But she was there for Rise, Rule, *and* Peak. Three months. Maria had noticed, of course —someone of her station could not miss *that*. But it had not seemed to be a problem at first. None of the other maids reported odd behavior or brought any concerns up. The Countess, as per usual, took the reports that she had not left her room, asked a couple of questions regarding meals and attitude, and sent Maria on her way.

Today was the first time in months Maria had been called on by the young Miss, and stat sickness is unheard of for Common Classes —it usually took ten points in a single attribute to cause it. For Common, that meant ten Levels —but for Uncommon that could be as few as two Levels if the Class was specialized enough. Maria had to report this. Another odd thing was that Eunora had Awakened at the beginning of Rise, Maria was sure of it. That means Eunora waited until after Young Lord Raphael came to see her.

Maria found it bizarre Raphael had advised her, but the other Awakened children had both taken guidance from Lina, their Governess. And Eunora always had clung to the other Dawns —despite her quiet nature, she always went out of her way to play in the vicinity of her siblings. And Lina *had* been on vacation starting the second week of Rise. She wasn't set to be back until the third week of Break

Soon enough, Maria had traversed the entirety of the estate and took a moment to straighten her apron and run a Skill over her outfit.

[Midsummer Breeze]

The deep violet fabric fluttered with the wind, and any stray hairs, bits of dust, and even a light smudge lifted and flew away from Maria. She had to straighten her bright white apron once more, cursing herself for forgetting she needed her Skill *after* already mundanely tidying herself.

Taking a deep breath, Maria shifted her stature. Her shoulders straightened, and Maria went from a demure maid to an ice queen, her eyes sharpened, and her hands settled behind her back. Her eyes settled on the guard outside the door, a Knight of the Dawn, who had averted his eyes as Maria had righted herself. Now he was looking back at her. She didn't smile.

"The Hands of Dawn work diligently to carve the Day."

Maria's voice was lined with power, and she felt the ice of her mana fill the air. The guard nodded and turned towards the door. With Strength, he knocked. Once. Twice. Three times he rapped his knuckles on the door. The sound reverberated through the hall, shaking a nearby portrait hung just a smidge too loose. Maria fought the urge to scold the guard. A breath later, the door swung open, and a man in a violet butler's uniform beckoned her inside.

"The Dawn beckons her Hand, as the Shining Day beckons the Everlasting Dawn."

The familiar voice filled Maria's ears, and as the door slammed behind her, she lowered into a kneeling position, one hand spread over her heart in a subtle salute.

"My Lady," Maria bowed her head before Countess Mallorica Dawn.

"Lift your head and rise."

The woman behind the desk had a head of black curls and blue eyes so deep they were nearly indigo. The Lady of Red Daybreak. Her very presence radiated power. Maria felt her mana spike in response.

"Yes, my liege."

Maria stood swiftly, meeting the Countess' eyes steadily.

"Report."

"As the Hand assigned to Eunora Dawn, I would like to report her Awakening and Class selection."

The Countess nodded slightly in acknowledgment and waved her hand back toward the door.

"Very well. I will call upon—"

"Pardon me, my Lady," Maria's voice remained calm, despite her fear, "But that is not all."

Mallorica leaned forward onto her previously held-out hand, a scowl on her face, "Continue."

"At the beginning of Rise, Eunora Dawn Awakened," Maria reiterated —as, for some reason, the Countess seemed to have been unaware of the Awakening, "But it appears she just chose her Class."

Mallorica's brows raised in surprise, "But it is Peak."

"Yes, my Lady." Maria nodded, "But there is a more pressing issue."

"Well? Out with it."

"It appears she is suffering from stat sickness."

"Eunora? Eunora Dawn?"

"Yes, my Lady."

"My daughter Eunora?"

"Yes?"

"The one who was supposed to Awaken this week?"

Maria understood then and winced.

"No, my Lady."

The Countess let out a breath-

"She has already Awakened. Again, in Rise."

"What has she been doing for three months?"

"Well—"

"And why have I been unaware?"

"Again—"

"And *stat sickness?*"

"Yes—"

"Summon her to me. Immediately."

Another wince from Maria.

"About that—" Maria took a sharp intake of breath as Mallorica's gaze grew baleful, "She has refused to leave her room."

"So she is sulking. Very well. Allow her to have a few days. How long has it been so far? A day? Two?"

Maria felt her heartbeat pick up, "Since Rise."

"I see—" Mallorica's brows furrowed as she processed Maria's words, "Since Rise?"

"Yes."

It was a long, silent moment before Mallorica tapped her nails along the wood of her desk. Presumably, deep in thought about what this meant for her daughter. Maria hoped she wouldn't decide that it was *her* responsibility to have made sure that the young Miss was leaving her room.

"What happened in Rise?" The solid voice of the Countess brought Maria back to reality.

"Nothing out of the ordinary according to the regular maids —I myself simply found she stopped calling upon me for morning meals."

At her words, a heavy air settled on the room. The Lady of Red Daybreak was unable to control her aura. Maria found it difficult to maintain her calm facade, a bead of sweat forming on her brow. It took everything she had to remain standing with her back straight.

Mallorica hit her palm against the desk, "It ends today. Dawns do not cower, or sulk, or whatever that *child* is doing."

Maria felt a lump in her throat, "My Lady?"

"What?"

"What about the stat sickness?"

Mallorica leaned back, crossing her arms, "I'll deal with that later. Her sulking ends in the morning, once the worst of it has passed."

And like that, the Countess took her aura under her control. Maria nearly collapsed in relief, but was able to kneel in acknowledgment.

"Yes, my liege."

The Countess had already gone back to marking a stack of papers on her desk when she spoke a final time, "Dismissed."

Forcing her way up, Maria steadily made her way out of the office, focusing on one step in front of the other. As soon as the door was closed behind her and she had made it around a corner —out of view of the Knight— she leaned her back up against the wall. Maria was not so weak that she would react this way to just anyone. She was well into her Tier 2 Uncommon Class. The strength of the Countess was well documented. She had served in the Queen's Guard in No Man's Land after all. But to live through it was always a trying endeavor.

With that thought, Maria pulled herself together and went back to being an average maid.

Mallorica, however, stewed for a while longer. If she were to say what it was she was feeling, *concern* is not what she would label it. Children are the affairs of lesser women. Women who are not pledged to serve their Queen and country. Women who are ordinary. She has led war bands in No Man's Land, has sat at negotiations with the King of Quoral, has sat beside the monarchs of Maeve as both a friend and confidant. Mallorica Dawn is anything but [Common]. She is the Duchess of Daybreak. The Countess of Dawn. She is the highest-ranked woman in Maeve after the Queen herself —the fifth highest-ranked overall if you pull in the rest of the Royal family. Thus, what Mallorica was feeling was irritation. Indignation. Dissatisfaction.

A child of the Dawn locking themselves away is unacceptable.

Not to mention the stat sickness. It's rare for a child to level up immediately, though not unheard of. So it's possible she is [Uncommon]. However, Mallorica had a suspicion that Eunora had somehow unlocked a [Rare] Class. Mallorica gave a feral smile —if that was true, Eunora would be more powerful than all of her siblings. Even Mallorica herself had not Awakened to a [Rare] Class.

As quickly as it appeared, her smile turned into a scowl. Eunora, despite being Mallorica's daughter, had taken the coward's way. Unacceptable. Even the possibility of a [Rare] Class was not enough to dampen her disapproval. After all, what use is the Class if the one who possesses it is useless themselves?

No. Eunora needs to learn how blessed she is to be of the Dawn. And how those blessings mean responsibility. Mallorica herself had always understood such things. She had always been the strongest of her siblings, the brightest, the most dutiful. And so, she came to a decision.

One way or another, she would find out what Eunora was made of. Be it sand or be it stone.

Chapter Seven

A Hero By Any Other Name

Peak of Autumn, Week 4, Day 4

I woke up to a vivid world impaling me. Even in the early morning light, I could make out the finer details of my room that even after months I had never noticed. From the smooth transition of paint to the small crack by the baseboard caused when I fell yesterday. Now, I saw the details, processed them, stored them, but they simply *were*. I didn't need to focus on them any more than I needed to focus on the wall to know it was a wall. Through the window came the green light of the moon, Revel. Its monstrous size provided an equal amount of light, but the hue was unsettling enough that I had a hard time forcing myself back to sleep.

Uncovering my body, I felt *strong*. I felt *alive*. My muscles, my heart, my hair, my skin –I was brimming with vitality. It was hard to hate this world when my body simply felt good. Running my hands across my arms, I could feel muscles hiding beneath a child's body. Making my way to a mirror, I studied myself. I was still in my nightgown from the day before, barefooted, and with my hair held back in a messy braid. Perhaps, had I not outwardly changed, I would have felt more at ease. But as it was, there was a gentle glow beneath my skin –not of magic or other such mysticism. No. It was the glow of a healthy child. I grit my teeth. After months of barely sustaining myself, of floundering, of refusing to thrive, simply accepting a Class had healed my bodily woes. No longer was I undersized and scrawny, drowning in the fabric of my nightgown, but now my body was lithe and looked as if I was the sort to spend every waking moment running in the woods, or riding dressage, or simply *playing.* The physical stats I had gained caused me to change. Now I was more like in *elsewhere.*

I felt my stomach roll, and I swallowed.

I wish I could say that seeing my body in such a state and feeling the way it was impacting my mind, I felt a renewed sense of wonder. That it gave me the drive to become strong. The truth was that being in this new land made me feel empty –no. *Angry.* The Eunora from before my awakening was hopeful, she was intelligent, and she wanted to make the Dawn family proud -even if that mattered little to the rest of the family. But she was cripplingly shy and woefully neglected. Memories of *elsewhere* brought me thoughts of warm embraces, of loving words, of striving to better myself, of a support system. I had wanted to be the best me I could be –for myself and my loved ones.

But now they were gone. Or I was. Worlds away. As I stared out the window up at Revel, tears pricked at the back of my eyes. The green moon, taking up a quarter of the sky, had a blue ring surrounding it. It was *foreign*, even now. Even after all this time. The fact that I felt strong made it worse, not better. I would rather be withered.

Down below my window laid the hedge maze —now a cacophony of reds and oranges painted the hedges leaves, rather than the vibrancy of spring. Fall was in full swing, after all. Perhaps had Eunora —no, *me, had I* been born in spring, with the life it brought to the world, I would be feeling hopeful. This view made me want to lay in a pile of fallen brown leaves and burrow beneath them to hide from the world. Perhaps one day, if I left this room, I would do just that.

Perhaps that day was today. I placed my hand on the window, stretching my fingers in anticipation and trepidation both. Then a knock resounded throughout my room, followed by a brief pause before the door flung open to reveal a woman twice my height with looks that foretold my future.

Light flooded my room as I took in the woman. Thick black curls and eyes so blue they were nearly indigo. A dress of the finest linen dyed the perfect shade of pink to mimic the light of dawn. Indigo embroidery to match the woman's fierce expression. Her curls, both untamed and under control, were held back from her face with a white tiara.

Mother. I could feel Eunora's—my own yearning for the woman. She was unmistakable. She was beautiful and proud and *strong*. She looked young, mid-thirties, perhaps that wasn't so young to most —let alone to a child, but this was the Lady of the house.

This was Countess Mallorica Dawn, the [Lady of Red Daybreak].

Despite the depths of my psyche clawing for her attention, her love, the part of me that lived remembered Raphael. How he hadn't known when I'd Awakened. How this woman had not bothered to pay attention.

Looking over at her from the window, I met her gaze, rage beginning to boil within my veins. There was nothing to fear from her, not truly. She was strong, yes. She had a presence, also true. But still. She will not strike me down for nothing.

"Eunora, daughter," A knife wrenched into my heart at her words, at her cold tone, at the smile that played on her severe face, "I believe we need to discuss your behavior."

81

A moment passed. Then another. I bit the inside of my cheek.

I still did not speak.

Mother didn't even look uncomfortable as she walked over to the sofa in my room and sat. She laid her hands in her lap as she ran her eyes over my body, whether she could tell a difference was lost on me.

"Well, at least you're out of bed." The disapproval in her voice shook me more than I was expecting, and I had to rush to catch the thread of anger that was quickly giving way to a flood of old emotions. Emotions that were no longer *mine*.

*This woman, no matter how I call her, she is not my mother. She never could be. I **have** a mother.*

"I am." My voice was clipped, harsh, tougher than the Countess. I couldn't adjust it, nor did I want to.

"I heard—" the Countess flicked her eyes from me to the sofa opposite her and back to me, "that you have not left this room since Rise."

Straightening my back, I turned fully towards her and took a single step, saying nothing. I wanted to scream, to tell her I would not be explaining to her why, to make her understand she had to *go. Not for me, but for Eunora, the original. You shouldn't be here with me. I am not the one who yearns for your love, Countess.*

"Were you a peasant, you would have starved, rotted away from disease, or dehydrated." The Countess said this so casually, with a humor that did not fit her, that I took a sharp breath, "You are fortunate to be a Dawn, Eunora."

82

I bit my cheek harder, still yet to taste the copper of blood. Still yet to have the pain ground me.

Am I supposed to say 'thank you'? Nausea forced me to swallow once again.

"You are too young, and too high-bred, to be this way. To be—" The Countess actually *did* sound sincere, at least in her irritation. Maybe such a thing could be born out of love, but it was more than likely I was an inconvenience. Either way, she eventually found the words she was looking for, "To be so degenerate. We've let you be for a while. It's time for you to stop this."

Ah, there it was.

I felt my outrage pour over, there was no more room in my small body for the feeling. It tinged the edge of my eyes and picked up my heartbeat.

You didn't even know! Eunora is **g o n e**. *She is gone, and I have taken her place, and you never even came to check why I hadn't left the room!*

Through my fog of anger, I was only able to get out, "Let me be?"

At the Countess' cold expression, I knew the answer was a resounding, *Yes.* She considered her inaction -no, her *ignorance* to be a passive allowance of my actions.

Now, when I bit the inside of my cheek, the taste of copper seeped out.

"Why?"

The Countess' brows rose, "Why *what,* Eunora?"

"Why should I leave this room?" Meeting the Countess' eyes was too much, and I had to look away, the sharpness was shifting something within me.

Unbidden, memories flitted forward. Of the Countess hushing the Count, of her ordering the Staff, of the siblings lining up to greet her on formal occasions. I knew she was Countess Dawn. But she is not just that — because she is *of* the Dawn. A true-born daughter just like me. From representing the County to the Queen to dominating in wars, she is a terrifying woman.

"Are you saying the reason you've not left your room is because there was no reason to?"

Looking down at my hands, I was mildly surprised they were clenched so tightly. *Maybe Eunora controls more of me than I thought.*

I nodded without looking back to the Countess.

"What about our family? Your classes? Leveling up?"

"I don't care about those things."

I still hadn't looked back.

"None of them? Not even us?"

I bit my lip to stop a snort from escaping but nodded my head.

After a pause, she spoke. This time my mother's voice was hard, not offended - not really, simply stern, "If none of these things interest you, then I will be the reason you leave this room."

The Countess paused, turning her head towards the window briefly before standing and focusing her gaze back on me, "Eunora, I am sending you to the west -to the

84

far reaches of Maeve. I am making a decision for the good of the Dawn. You will live in the borderlands."

Confused, I looked up to her, but she continued without wavering, "While there, you will learn what is required of a member of house Dawn -you will have many options. Study diligently in your classes to become a proper noble, train your body to become a member of the Conclave's knights, or continue to remain ignorant of the world. There will be knights, magicians, and scholars to guide you. Pick one path —or dabble in all three. *Or* continue to fester. You will remain in the West until your coming of age."

"You… are you *exiling* me?"

"I believe this is a win for both of us, Eunora. I will have you out of this room and on a path other than isolation - *whatever* that path may be. Meanwhile, you will have ten years to decide what matters to you –without having to be bothered by the rest of us."

The Countess had a distasteful expression as she gestured to herself and the estate around her, but her voice could not be said to be filled with anything more than authority. With that, she turned away from me and made her way out of the room, pausing at the doorway to look over at me, "Remember, the Dawn family is a pillar of Maeve. Even allowing you to be cast out to the borderlands is a concession. You leave next week."

As the door closed behind her, a green system notice filled my vision.

[Congratulations! Mental Fortitude is now level 4!]

"This system is sadistic," I bit out.

I was going to lay back down and sleep until I was forced to leave. But right as I went to fall back into my pillows, I found myself standing and walking over to the window.

Suddenly, the thought of leaving the room wasn't so daunting —not if I was being forced to do so already. With a deep breath, I unlatched the window pane and pushed it open. In the garden, leaves rustled with the wind and birds chirped overhead. Occasionally, I could see a small animal flitting from hedge to hedge. It made me want to feel even half as alive as the hedge maze below.

So, I pushed the window even wider. The window ledge was the perfect height to sit upon and stare out over the gardens. The perfect place to feel the breeze across my face. But I didn't sit on the ledge —I stood on it. And I jumped.

If it had been the Eunora from *before*, even the second story would have hurt her. Broken a bone, or sprained an ankle. But I had mid-level Vitality, Strength, and Perception. So, I simply landed, bending my knees as my feet sunk into the soft soil.

Sliding through the gap between two bushes, I stepped onto the brick walkway. Lightly, I began walking to the center of the garden.

There was a cloying anger in my heart, burning me. Indignation and outrage and a burning desire for the emptiness I had felt for the past months. But, still, I walked through the maze.

From my room, I had memorized the paths within the half-dead hedge maze that surrounded the central fountain. A quick right, go past the next intersection, a left just to follow a hedge that goes into a u-turn, follow the hedge straight, another right, and a final left at the last intersection, lead me to a circular opening with a large fountain in the middle. Four stone benches surrounded it, set in between the four entrances to the clearing. All four were covered in hedged archways, but one had more ornate decorations. This was the entry to the main courtyard — *and where the Dawns held garden parties.* Memories unhelpfully supply context to the world around me. The archways were decorated by Dawn Roses -those that hold all the colors of a sunrise, a pale orange base with petals that shifted into a soft pink and were rimmed with a bright red, these flowers decorated all key entry and exit points on the estate.

I sat on the edge of the fountain, swinging my feet right above the water, and stared up at the statue that overlooked the hedge maze. It was of the hero Countess Lyla Dawn, and it was carved with such detail that I often wondered if it was going to wake up one day and start walking around. The statue of Lyla was adorned like all pieces focusing on her were -her long hair was pulled up and through a warrior's helm, the helm itself had two horns protruding off the sides and sweeping back away from her face. The statue had her in her standard leather armor, the tasseled skirt flowed to her knees, the greaves and bracers she wore had two blades protruding out of them. It was said that being behind Lyla's guard was just as bad as being out of it because no matter where you were, there was always a blade ready to devour you. The sculptor had given her the signature spear she was said to have wielded in wartime, with one arm by her side and the other grasping the haft. Lyla Dawn was often lauded as the savior of the kingdom during the Hilled Wars centuries ago.

After seeing her statue, I had wondered what great feat she had accomplished, what mythic class she must have had. The answer was a bit mundane, my mind supplied once more that her class was a combat class, undisclosed, but her fame lies in that she collapsed the supply line of the Ylle, one of the larger Hill Tribes. After waiting two weeks, she and her company attacked the malnourished troops of the Ylle and took away the strategic outcropping they were occupying. In the end, she was yet another noble who didn't really care about the collateral damage she caused. To this day, the Ylle lands are unable to be safely inhabited due to Lyla destroying a mountain pass and poisoning a key water supply. Some time later, the refugees from the Hill Tribes found their way to Maeve and caused a civil war in the process. One book Eunora read featured a historian that endearingly referred to that timeframe as 'the Dawn of a broken Maeve'. *That did wonders for the Dawn name, I'm sure.* Even still, she was lauded as the great divide between the Nobles and the Queensmen.

Taking a breath, I met the statue's bored-looking eyes, "Lyla, how did you make it through the war?"

As if the Gods were answering on her behalf, a strong wind filled the courtyard -bringing with it several of the Dawn Roses. One of which drifted across my face, settling onto my lap. Gingerly picking up the rose, I held it in both my hands and let a small smile form.

"You know, back home, these roses had a different name -they were called the Love and Peace Rose," I brought the bud up to my face and inhaled, "I never saw them in person, just the hand-dyed roses at the local store. I don't know if they fit our legacy, but they *are* beautiful."

Taking another moment, I looked back to Lyla and slid from the fountain's edge into the water. On an adult, it may have been mid-calf depth, but it reached past my knees and drenched the bottom quarter of my nightgown. I waded to the center of the fountain and climbed to the pedestal that the statue was standing on. Reaching the farthest I could, my arm barely stretched to her collarbone -but it was enough. I let go, letting the rose that was in my palm sit atop a precarious ledge right above the statue's chest.

"May the Dawn ever rise, Lyla."

As I climbed back down, the wind returned and caused me to shiver. It wasn't a particularly cold day, but the wind tickled the wetness soaking my dress. It may have been pushing it to trudge through water in a thin nightgown -even if I did have five times the Vitality of other kids my age.

As the suns fully rose, and Revel settled down in the far horizon, I watched as the light cascaded down the statue. I stood back and watched as the rose I had placed stayed on Lyla's chest for an inordinate amount of time. Eventually, I sat on one of the stone benches and felt the coldness creeping up my legs from the wet nightgown. Somehow, it made me feel alive.

It wasn't until I began hearing voices approaching over an hour later that I got up and decided to head back to my room.

Chapter Eight

The Apathetic Dawn

Peak of Autumn, Week 4, Day 4

At the noise, I slid off the bench and slipped back down the path I'd taken before. I wondered if this was the work of [Otherworldly]. Fateful encounters were an unfortunate effect of the Skill. Would this qualify? It was likely one of the older Dawns —Raphael or Evelyn. The morning was still too fresh for the younger Dawns to be up and about.

Navigating the labyrinthine hedges, I took a moment to listen once more. In the distance, I heard indistinct laughs and whispers. I couldn't tell exactly how far they were, but with my new Perception and the low volume of their voice, I figured I had some time to slip away.

"[Silent as a Shadow]"

The Skill hummed out of me, and I felt a shock of cold pool in my stomach before dispersing across my body. Unlike the chill of the water from earlier, this cold did not cause me to shiver or flinch. This cold was a comfort. The world desaturated around me, the colors of mid-morning becoming indistinguishable from the browns of the hedges. Even the sounds of small critters had faded around me. It felt as if I was walking through a drawing. It was a reminder of my own power.

Power, I scoffed at the thought. *I have no power. Not in this life.*

As if in acceptance, I could feel somewhere inside of me [Otherworldly] had retracted. Whatever its original distance, I could now feel its passive existence inches from my skin. I let out a breath I hadn't realized I'd been holding. In the periphery, the voices faded into the distance as I slipped through the hedges to make my way back to my room.

I felt [Silent as a Shadow] end gradually, colors and sound returning to the world around me as I peered up at my window. Looking up at the second story, where the window frame hung open still, I realized I had made a mistake.

How am I supposed to get back up?

Immediately, I tried lowering myself into a crouch and jumping up. That did not work. I only made it eight feet, roughly double my height, before I slid down the wall with my hands scrambling for purchase. Fortunately, my Dexterity allowed me to position myself to land safely — but that didn't mean comfortably. I had scratched my palms against the rough texture of the wall as I caught myself from rolling an ankle on landing.

I tried to use [Quick Calculation] to get me to a spot where I could jump from or a tree that was close enough to scale, anything that meant I could solve this problem here and now. I swallowed as every result returned a failure.

Unless... I used [Quick Calculation] one more time to determine how much mana I had left in me.

It might work. The laws of magic in Gargantua were different than in the before. In *elsewhere*, magic was controlled with finesse and Will —it was more intuitive and free form. Here it requires contracts and foci and *work*. Skills didn't require any of that, though. Skills were abilities that worked like in *elsewhere*.

"[Weave of Darkness]"

Once again, the ice-cold prick of mana funneling into a Skill filled me. Unlike with [Silent as a Shadow], when the mana disbursed, it focused on my hands and left my body —forming a ball of pitch-black yarn. Strictly speaking, I hadn't directed it to be the color of Shadowless Night, but my heart had desired it, and thus that is what was produced. Similar to how I knew I would need at least 45 yards of yarn for what I wanted to do. I was confident the ball of shadow was that length.

Unlike my other Skills, I had practice with [Weave of Darkness] —it felt comfortable to use, and I had been able to understand its limits firsthand rather than from [Inspect]. And even if I had not understood it so well, I really did not want to go through the whole of the estate to get back to my room. In fact, I cannot understate how much I hated that idea.

Gripping the ball of yarn in my hands, I took a breath. Everything told me what I wanted to do was possible. I could do it. I held out a single hand and spoke. I didn't actually know what tensile strength meant, but [Inspect] had said it was 572, which did not strike me as a small number. The real trick would be getting the ball wrapped around the window frame several times so I could use it to climb. And hoping then that the frame could hold me. With Strength, I wasn't sure if that came with weight — and my memories told me nothing.

Unraveling the ball, I used the loose end to tie around my wrist. Pulling out enough yarn to reach the top of the window frame and then some, I began to aim. Right as I angled my arm up, swung, and released, I watched as the yarn hooked over the frame and began to fall. I felt a small smile bloom at my success and went to grab the ball of yarn to do it again.

"What are you doing?"

I jumped at the voice, my hand clenched on the yarn and spun on my heel. I had been so engrossed in the endeavor I hadn't really been paying attention to the world at large. But now I was met with a boy barely older than me, with blue eyes that matched my own. The first Dawn I had met after being shoved into this world.

Theodore Dawn.

As he addressed me, I felt the old Eunora well up inside. The feeling of smallness that Theodore brought up in her was crushing, and my heart ached at the thought of such a young girl feeling so unwanted. Theodore was never cruel with his words, but his actions spoke of his apathy. Eunora had known that she was not as smart as Theodore, who could memorize books even prior to Awakening. She knew that he thought as such too.

But something irked me, a thread of a thought. Everyone else had thought that Rise 8th had been just another day. Raphael and the Countess confirmed it. Even Maria had unintentionally confirmed as such with her actions. But Theodore had come to wake me up. Granted, afterwards, he hadn't come to check on me. But he had come. I had nearly forgotten in the face of everything that had happened. Theodore had never done that before.

Why had he come?

Even now, why was he bothering to talk to me?

What does he want?

"What are you *doing?*" He repeated emphatically.

I looked up at the window, with a single strand of yarn wrapped around the extended frame, then to the yarn still sitting on the ground, then down to my nightgown, before finally looking at Theodore again.

"Nothing."

Disbelief crossed his face as he looked from me to the window.

"Nothing?"

"Nothing that concerns you."

Unlike with Raphael, Theodore never came across as a bully. There was simply hurt and inadequacy spawned by his indifference. That was as damning as Raphael to me. Even children should have limits on how they treat others. Anger and disdain surged within me. *This whole family is rotten*, I thought, *maybe exile is exactly where I should be.*

"It's barely morning, what are you doing throwing a…" he narrowed his eyes as he focused his gaze around where I was standing, "Ball of yarn?"

I took a slow breath in and released a slow breath out, "Nothing-"

"Nothing that concerns me," he interrupted in a droll voice and crossed his arms, "Yeah, all right, whatever."

Despite growing quiet, he didn't move to go. And I didn't speak. He just stood, scrutinizing me. Seconds passed. I glanced back at the yarn, debating if I should just continue what I was doing.

"I heard Raphael came by."

Yeah, I decided, *I'll just ignore him.* I picked up the ball of yarn and passed it from hand to hand, unraveling enough of it to reach the window frame again. As I did so, I heard Theodore uncross and cross his arms.

"Did you tell him your [Class]?"

Ignore him. He isn't worth your time.

I threw the ball, another smooth arc over the window frame. A success. This time, there was no smile. I went over to the ball and picked it up.

"Considering you've been moping for ages, how horrid was it?"

He knew —I could feel it. He didn't mean days, the emphasis on 'ages' was too much. He knew my birthday was Rise 8th.

Ignore him. Just. Ignore him. He still didn't come back. It's been months.

I walked another few steps and began unraveling more yarn. The ball was a quarter of its original size by then. Holding the two loose strings to stop them from joining the ball in the air, I aimed once again.

"What? Was your only choice a [Common] [Class]?"

Ignore him.

The ball flew just over the top of the frame and began unraveling mid-air. As it fell, the ball came completely undone, and the final string hung loosely from the frame. It was dragging lightly on the ground and moving easily with the breeze. I went over and grabbed it, stepping back so all three strings were taught between my hand and the frame.

*572 TS * 3 = 1,716 TS,* flicked in my head, and I sighed. If it wasn't enough before, hopefully, it was now. I could feel Eunora's brother staring at me expectantly, waiting for me to give in and answer him.

"Go away, Theodore." I sighed.

I didn't even bother looking back at Theodore as I wrapped the ends of the strings around my waist —just small enough to secure them. And grabbed the higher-up yarn. Then I began a rope climb. It was easier than I was expecting, hooking my hand around the strings and pulling my body up. In fact, it was so easy, when I was up high enough to hook my foot in the rope to steady myself, I hardly even needed to do so. I did, of course, do so — because I'm not an idiot, and it's safer to hook my foot too. Why did I want to do this *safer*? Because, as I have said once, twice, thrice before, despite being stuck here, I don't really relish the thought of being dead. Even if being alive sucks.

Once I tugged myself up into the wide windowsill I looked back down to Theodore, who had an inscrutable expression on his usually bland face.

"Why are you still here?" I shook my head lightly, a scowl replacing my own bland expression, "Go away."

Pulling in the yarn, I began rolling it back up into a ball. The interesting bit about [Weave of Darkness] was that it *permanently* summoned shadowed thread. Thus, I was able to have quite a bit of knitted animals below my bed. And coasters. And a scarf. Perhaps I would summon a ball of Shadowless Day and [Weave] them together. Again. Theodore occasionally called out to ask me about my [Class], but otherwise stayed where he was while I spent minutes gently unlooping the yarn from the window frame to make sure it wasn't snagged or snapped. Though, after how easily I had used it to climb up, I was doubtful that a rough tug would be enough to sever the yarn. But I wasn't sure. I was careful anyway.

Once I was finished and had a relatively neat ball of yarn sitting next to me, I closed the window without looking at Theodore. He was not my issue. If he wanted to come harass me again, he would have to get through a locked door now. With a huff, I tossed the ball onto my bed and went into the bathroom. I was *trying* to bathe more often, to prevent myself from physically festering any longer. After being trapped in my bed for a majority of the day before, it had been two days since I'd bathed. Which meant now was as good a time as any.

Looking at my face in the mirror, I was shocked once again by the Vitality that fueled my skin. No longer were my cheeks sunken or my eyes dull, my skin was fresh and soft and free of the paleness that had haunted me since I refused to eat regularly. My muscles felt free and I undid my braids with deft fingers, faster and easier than two days prior. I wondered, briefly, if [Weaving] would help me make better braids. Within me, the Skill confirmed it would by sending images of transferable knots and woven patterns that would allow me to decorate my hair.

Soon enough, I was back to laying atop my bed in a fresh nightgown with loose hair. I did not want to braid my hair. Or eat lunch. Or get off the bed.

But I did. I ate an apple-like fruit with purple and orange skin, and I said hello to Maria. I used a slightly more complicated braid on my hair —just a single step above the basic— it required five strands instead of three, and it turned out just lovely enough that I found myself with a mildly improved mood. And I did all these things off the bed.

Despite the rude awakening this morning, or perhaps because of it, I had had a rather okay day. I frowned. *If I ignored Theodore popping up.*

Chapter Nine

In the Name of Comfort

Peak of Autumn, Week 4, Day 4

Exile, that's the name of the game. I released a breath I had been holding. It was afternoon, and so much —*too much*, had happened in a day. But maybe that was the nature of my presence now. Too much. Too soon. I had wanted to take a small step into this world on my own terms, and traversing through an empty hedge maze had seemed perfect. But I overstayed my welcome in the garden, narrowly avoiding a group but still being caught by Theodore. It felt like a plunge in the ocean instead of a dip in the shallow end. And I was tired of being taken off guard. Now that leaving was an option, I can admit I wanted it desperately. Wherever the Countess sent me, I wanted to go —as long as there were no other Dawns around me to dredge up the old Eunora's insecurities.

Even if that meant the Borderlands. The *Borderlands*.

I felt the anxiety of Eunora well up within me. This body had never left the estate, let alone traversed Maeve. She had been a child. She knew such places were dangerous, that they were where men and women made names for themselves through the monsters they hunted. This world was not peaceful or kind —but neither was *elsewhere*.

And maybe that's a blessing that this world is similar in such a way. Maybe it's a comfort. Am I looking for comfort?

The bright light of both suns filled my room, and I frowned. That wouldn't do. Not if I truly *wanted* to be comforted. It was an act of will, then, when I rose from where I was laid out and roughly closed the curtains. One set, two, and the final third set clanking as I dragged the fabric across the bar. The room was not fully dark, not in the way night is dark, but it was overlaid with gray, and it was taking time for my eyes to adjust.

Before that could happen, I felt a whisper leave me.

"[Shadow Manipulation]"

The ice-cold feeling of mana spiked through my body and shot out of me, suffusing the air like an aura and then swiftly dispersing.

At first, I thought nothing had happened. The shadows had remained still. They had remained but an overlay.

It was as I let out a small breath that they came alive.

The shadows remained flat, and they did not grow, but wisps of darkness radiated off the base shadows now. And they were significantly darker the closer they were to me. I stared at the shadows connecting to the bottom of my feet and felt my will pour out of me. The darkness swelled and shifted, detaching from the objects the shadows were meant to mirror –leaving shades of grey where they had been. All the will in me focused on bringing the darkness to me, around me, surrounding me. It was unrefined, and despite the clarity of my mind, the blob of shadows that grew around me was amorphous. I reached a single hand out, grasping the solid darkness –only for my hand to pass through the incorporeal body.

I nearly hissed at the disappointment before another whisper left my body.

"[Shadow Conjuration]"

The ice-cold feeling of mana burst out of every pore on my body. It followed my will. The nature of the darkness surrounding me changed. The blob of incorporeal shadows pulsed once, twice, and then I could *feel* the darkness caressing my skin, shifting my dress like the wind, brushing the hair from my face. It was warmth, it was safety.

The darkness was a comfort I had thought I wanted.

My stomach roiled with grief once again. It was from *elsewhere*, memories of my life flooding me in a harsh tidal wave that I hadn't felt for weeks.

Heels clack down tiled halls, friends laughing as we walk, drinks in our hand as we move to a patio to overlook the Dome from one of our rooftops. Names I cannot remember but faces that are crisp in my mind, dark hair, and smile lines on one woman as she grabs me by the arm and drags me forward. Bangles clink as another, with short auburn hair and dark skin, catches my drink from spilling and takes the glass from my hand. A third woman, with blonde hair to match my own and a flowing white dress releases a laugh. She nearly trips, and I pulse my Will. Magic flows like a river out of me, and a bar of darkness appears to steady the blonde. I can hear her soft voice thanking me as she pulses her own WIll, summoning a yellow flame to dry the three drops that landed on her before they settled. Casual, soft, simple magic. But magic all our own.

I gasp as I come back to the present. Grief is overtaken by rage. I cannot fathom a world alone. I cannot stand it, even now, even after months have passed. I was stripped of my life, taken from my world, for a game I don't know how to play. A game I don't know how to win. A game I wished so thoroughly I could opt not to play. My mind spiraled with fury. The blood in my veins boiled at the very thought of the Gods. Of being given the same magic I had always possessed. It was a trick. A trap. Something meant to drag me further into this life. A constant meant to give me comfort, I was sure. Because it had almost *worked*. It was so ingrained in me that I nearly *forgot*. I nearly let my memories slide off, let them disappear into the ether.

In response to the anger in my veins, the fluid darkness rolled against my body violently. It separated into misshapen tendrils that wrapped around me, constricting me. Functioning as a weighted blanket I did not want, cutting me off from the light slinking in through the fabric of the curtains.

Or maybe I did want it.

This was *my* will. It had to be what I craved.

A creature comfort I needed so desperately that my mind willed it without my conscious decision.

I hated that it was working. The solid black darkness in my immediate surroundings made me feel as if I could be anywhere. I could be in a field with miles to go before civilization. I could be in *elsewhere*, standing at the center of a bedroom I could only access in my memories. I could be free from this world in the dark.

My breathing, shallow and choppy, slowly began to normalize, and I released the fists I was clenching so tightly it was surprising that I didn't break skin. I wanted to scream, but instead, I pushed the palm of my hand against my mouth and sobbed. I let the grief flow. I let the rage focus on the sense of loss it accompanied. I let the tears well and fall. I let it out.

And then, as time passed, I began taking deep breaths. I felt a numbness overtake me.

I had a notification.

[Congratulations! Mental Fortitude is now level 5! New features unlocked.]

Wiping my eyes, I snorted, dark amusement filling me.

"All you do, you stupid Skill, is feed off my pain, huh?"

It made me wonder if [Mental Fortitude] actually did anything, despite its claim. Or, perhaps, it simply was the difference of a razor's edge. That would explain the difference in leveling the Skill when compared to the others –[Mental Fortitude] may require extreme distress to grow, while it shaves a sliver of torment off. Then again, three months ago, I went unshowered for weeks at a time and only ate the bare minimum –whereas now, I was at least out of bed and cleaned up more often than not. So, maybe it was working.

Or maybe that's just the way grief works –it wrecks you until you find the strength to stand. The waves becoming more tolerable when they try to knock you back down, every attempt getting easier to resist.

The thought didn't stop the tears that were flowing freely once again from my eyes, but something broken inside of me understood that maybe this emptiness could give way. In time. And it helped me breathe easier.

As the last hiccups left me and the crying stopped in earnest, I felt the ache of my heart settle down. Not in a way that made it better but in a way that made me find my Will. In the dark, the shadows writhed and tightened around me as if to embrace me once more. And then they unfurled from around my body, opening me back up to see the dim room around me —still gray but without defined shadows.

I felt present in a way I hadn't before. I felt grounded. A part of me knew it was the comfort of the shadows, the familiarity seeping into my soul once again.

I took a breath, deep and slow. I let the air fill my lungs to capacity. I held the oxygen within me for one, two, three. Gently, I released. And as my breath left me, I focused on a single crude tendril of darkness.

Smaller. Finer. Smoother.

"Denser," I whispered the final command.

Collapsing in on itself, the crude lumps of the shadow tendril flattened as I pictured a cleaner shape. I felt the cold shock of mana leaving me again, and a sweat built as I focused my mind's eye on the shape I desired. But the shadow had obeyed. It continued shrinking and smoothing its harsh lines, creating a vine-like shape.

For a time.

Seconds later, it was with a snap and a shock of ice flooding my veins that I was forced to release my Skills. The shadows flooded away from me, racing to settle back into their natural state.

I was out of mana. That was the only answer, as an ache began to settle into the back of my mind. Every shift of the walls sent a new bolt of pain through the back of my head, and my instinct warned me I shouldn't try another Skill. An instinct that felt more like a plea to not be ignored than anything innocuous.

So, with shaking hands, I went back to the windows and gently pulled the curtains back open. What had felt like an eternity of sobbing —and then moments of comfort— turned out to be long enough for one of the suns to settle over the horizon. The light of day had begun to give way to the dark of night on the far end of the sky.

I was once again reminded I had no power. Not yet. I was still trapped as a child, but that could change with time. But there was another reminder that I was weak, and it came in the form of two notifications flooding my vision.

[Congratulations! Shadow Manipulation is now Level 2! Class experience applied!]

[Congratulations! Shadow Conjuration is now Level 2! Class experience applied!]

Chapter Ten

Magelights In My Eyes

Peak of Autumn, Week 4, Day 5

She gave me a day. A single day to myself. Then the Countess had my world upended.

I awoke to a soft knock on my door, which in and of itself was not unsettling. Then I was kept up by the gentle shaking of metal hinges that followed a half-breath pause. That, still, was not unusual. I have been keeping the door locked, after all. It was the distinct click of unlocking that caught me unaware. Snapping my head up, blue eyes met amber.

"Good morning, my Lady," Maria smiled softly as she held the door open —revealing several others behind her, "We are here to prepare you for your move."

What an irritating way to wake up –to someone pedantically calling exile a 'move' as if I was simply switching rooms to get a better view of the garden. What had been mildly alarming, waking up to the door rattling, had now become fuel for a bad mood. It did not help that the sea of faces behind Maria were unfriendly. They were hostile in the way strangers often are, in the way that a boss's petulant child makes good gossip, and workers will rally with complaints. And I am under no presumption that I am anything but such a child to them. Even Maria, whose eyes are always soft and whose work is consistently deft, likely thinks nothing more of me than someone she is paid to coddle. I would think the same, after all, were this *elsewhere*. I would not be the type to love a child that was not my own in all the ways that matter. I am not of Maria's blood, nor has she nursed me.

I am not overly compassionate, nor was the original, and Maria, though she is *nice,* she is not overly *kind.* She cares in the way someone who is well compensated is expected to, no more and no less. The understanding of that does not stop the phantom pains of loneliness from radiating from my heart, but they are remnants of a child's heart –not the heart I had covered in steel from *elsewhere.*

That has been one of the worst bits. Feeling aches stemming from emotions that have no place in my heart. Loneliness, inadequacy, *anxiety.* These are not who I *am.* Even now, as I look across the faces of the help, there are two emotions at war within me –contempt and uncertainty.

A voice, not as far down as I would like, whispers, *Why aren't you getting up? They are w a t c h i n g.* The voice is small, and it wavers as it speaks into my mind.

Then there is *me.* In a voice laced with disgust and outrage, the sound of my own voice thuds against my mind spitting vitriol. *Who cares what they think? Let them burn. They work for the Dawns. That is enough for them to be worthless.*

It is an odd thing to have two separate voices in your own head. And it is wholly unpleasant.

"The Countess gave me until next week," I ground out, fighting both voices back.

Maria gave me an indulgent smile, "Before you leave, yes."

"It has only been a day," I replied, my voice monotonous even to my own ears, unable to muster enough energy to fight –I could feel in my bones it was a losing battle.

"Yes, now we've less than a few days to prepare your items, my Lady," Maria's sickly sweet tone was enough to turn my mood from low to the bottom of the barrel.

I forced myself to roll over. I took five seconds. Five seconds to breathe and stare at the ceiling.

"I'm not yet dressed."

The silence was deafening, and when I glanced at Maria, her amber eyes were pitying. It was as if she was saying, *Yes, because that would definitely happen in its own time had we left you to it.* It was really a rather rude thing to say with her eyes.

"Very well, my Lady. Do you require aid to get ready, or shall we return in, say, the better part of an hour?"

I looked back to the ceiling as I spoke, "Can it not be two?"

"... it can be two."

"Fine, no, no aid, I'll be fine. Please leave."

Blessedly, they did. The door closed, and I breathed a sigh of relief. Finally tearing my eyes from the ceiling, I fought to stay awake –even though both suns were well into the sky, marking it as mid-morning at least. After exhausting my mana, I had slept like the dead.

A short time later, I was tying my hair back into two loose braids with soft marine ribbons. I had yet to wear anything other than a nightgown in the time I'd spent hidden in this room. And so it was time for proper clothes. All of which were in the pastel colors of dawn, from pinks to lavenders and periwinkles, and even some richer purples and indigos. I searched through the clothes for something neutral –a brown or grey. Instead, the closest I could find was a pale blue dress adorned with golden embroidery of the two suns revolving around each other. It had a soft yellow ribbon at the waist I could tighten and frills on the bottom of the long sleeves. The hem only went to my knees, so I slid on a pair of stockings matching the soft yellow ribbon. Even the shoes were in the colors of dawn –no browns, tan, or grey, not even black. So I slid into some soft blue leather boots that laced up past my ankles and went to the window.

I still felt I had time before the help would return. An abundance of time. *Do I want to remain here, waiting for their uncomfortable return?* The answer to that was a resounding *No. Not in the slightest.*

Back at the bed laid not one but two knit bunnies. One was the purple and silver rabbit that Eunora had knit over a span. The other was smaller and made of pitch-black yarn and iridescent eyes. That bunny had been *me.* I approached them both and held them up next to one another. The purple bunny was cruder, but I could feel the warmth radiating from within me when I looked into its eyes. Meanwhile, the black bunny had been a hand in the dark to keep me from insanity.

I carefully tucked the purple bunny into the basket below the bed and wrapped my arms around the black bunny. It would be my companion for the day.

"Let's head to the garden, Noir," I sighed.

Just as yesterday, I pushed open the window and jumped.

Even with the new clothes, I landed just as I had before, with the soft thud of my heels and the slight bend of my knees. Maybe I expected to feel something, and maybe I *did* feel something. It could be how the breeze felt fresher than the day before or how my muscles felt more limber after being used two days in a row. It could be how I was taking the sun on my skin or the chill in the air that was sharpening my breath. All of these were things that I hadn't noticed the day before. Things I had ignored or hated or refused to acknowledge. And maybe that was all the difference.

My heels dug into the ground, and I slipped between the hedges, finding my way to the brick walkway. Rather than returning to the statue of Lyla, I headed in the opposite direction –a memory of a memory guiding me along a familiar route.

"Come bunny, let's find somewhere nice to read," I whisper gently as my steps softly thud against the stone.

*It had been a long day of Eve pushing, prodding, and goading. She was right to, of course, I had been clinging to her, and she never asked for that. But her magelights were just so **pretty**. I couldn't help but stare. She wasn't wrong when she called me a nuisance.*

Rubbing my still stinging eyes, I glanced up over the hedge and caught sight of the window to my room. Between the curtains were two maids cleaning the glass panes. I should stay away until the afternoon to give them time to do their work.

The path away from the estate was filled with color – flowers bloomed in every bush and tree branch. There were crimson Sun Shines and indigo Star Flowers, there were the chartreuse Hearts of Sol, and the blush-colored Dovetails. As my feet padded along, I gripped my book tightly, grateful Eve's latest prank hadn't destroyed it. She had been practicing her spellwork by cousin Lyla, making her magelights change color as her tutor read the statue's story aloud. Eve had been meant to tie the color of her spell to the story's mood. Once she had spotted me staring, she had their brightness flare with such power that my vision went blurry.

It was a winding path that split off into different directions. The left path led to the side entrance of the barracks, the middle path would meander until it rejoined the left path at the training grounds, and the right path led to more garden. It would pass by several denser areas spotted with clearings meant for such things as mid-day reading trysts. I headed not for the first or second of these clearings but the third. It was in the hopes that no one would continue on so I could settle in and read a tale about Scylla and her Godtouched. This one was supposed to be one of the founding myths of Logos, the empire across the southern sea. It had taken ages before Lina allowed me to take it out of the library.

'Frivolous and unnecessary,' Her high-pitched voice had said, 'You should be focusing on your actual curriculum.'

But supposedly, this one has dragons. So I'd fought Lina for the better part of a month to prove I knew my writing and arithmetic well enough to be 'frivolous.' Of course, by fought, I mean I studied the books she had given me well into the night. When she declared I was 'acceptable' I politely slid <u>Scylla and her Tydes: A Story of Fortuitous Waves</u> towards Lina. With a disapproving huff, she slid it back and added more arithmetic books alongside it.

'I want this done within the month,' She had said.

*The books were difficult, with triple-digit addition and even multiplication. Still, reading about the Goddess of Luck's adventures in the mortal plane was worth it. She was among the few still worshipped in Maeve after the last Divine Revolution, and her history was so **cool**.*

Stepping off the garden path, I slid between one of the hedge archways. Behind the greenery was a small clearing lined with bushes blooming with some kind of lilac flower. There were two stone benches around a table and stepping stones leading toward the setup. But the moongrass that filled the clearing looked soft, with its green and blue speckled blades so lively, so I unwrapped the shawl from around my shoulders and sat atop it.

The memory flitted through my mind between one step and the next, a memory so visceral I could still feel the soft moongrass beneath me as I sat and read. Words unknown to me had become familiar, and I gave a small sigh. Memories with Eunora's essence were different than the dreams that had plagued me during the integration. That had been facts, it was truly *just* the memory. But walking around, weaving, and re-performing things she had done unlocked something new. It unlocked her *thoughts*. It reminded me that while I was in control of Eunora's mind and body, we were one now. I was she, and she was me. Nausea filled me.

I looked at the bunny I was holding, a recreation of the bunny from Eunora's memory. Noir was pitch black with shining eyes, the yarn reflecting the light into a myriad of colors. It was the opposite of the purple bunny Eunora had carried, with its dark eyes and nose.

It was unlike anything pre-Awakening Eunora could have created.

The garden itself was just like Noir –what had been colorful in memory was dim in reality. As I found myself following the path towards the moongrass clearing, I wondered about this choice. I wondered if the Gods would approve. Stepping backwards, to where the path began splitting, I closed my eyes. I felt the breeze run across my cheeks.

I opened my eyes and spoke.

"[Sophism]"

Chapter Eleven

Swarming Shadows

Peak of Autumn, Week 4, Day 5

Time slowed around me, my mind speeding up. The dull garden, with its browning leaves, remained unchanged. At first, I was confused. No white overlay showed the path of Order; no crimson light showed the path of Chaos. It was simply a garden headed toward the peak of fall.

Of course, I hissed in my head, *because why would a Skill ever work to my benefit?*

Within a breath, I had deactivated [Sophism] and pulled up the Skill description. The world sped up —my body along with it.

[Sophism: You have attracted the attention of the God of Order, Brel. In order to help guide you to the proper path, Brel has gifted you the ability to see Paths to Order and Chaos. The skill will help your rationalization of events and will occasionally give you direction on which is the Path of Order and which is the Path of Chaos. This skill is directly affected by your Perception stat. Whenever you are making a decision, your perception of time will slow but your processing speed will not. One second can be slowed by a factor of 5 for every 1 Perception. The effectiveness is increased per level.]

The rich green of the System greeted me and I felt something hook itself around my heart. Despite the Dawns denying me the ability to wear the colors of life, I still had this. A type of disobedience that can never be taken from me.

"Occasionally?" I ground out, burying my face in my hands, "Will *occasionally* give direction?"

A choked laugh escaped me. It was ridiculous, and my laugh was a harsh thing, born of rage rather than humor.

"This is insane," I groaned, "The damn God didn't even give me something I could intentionally use. Not in the way he implied. Fine."

Closing my Status, I returned my attention to the garden, stepping back down the third path.

"I'll just do what I was going to do anyway."

I passed the first clearing, then the second, before coming to the third clearing —the one from the memory, with the moongrass that had looked so plush. But that memory was from spring, when life had returned to the garden. Now the blue-green speckled grass was yellow with brown speckles. Rather than sitting down on the moongrass, I made my way to the stone setup and sat atop the table. Crossing my legs, I looked around. The edges of the clearing were thick with dying hedges and wilted leaves. Two matching statues were displayed upon pillars on either side of the entry. They depicted the first sun high in the air and the second sun half risen. Another reminder of the Dawn. I forcibly shut off that line of thinking –I could already feel rage boiling beneath my skin as my mind flicked back to the memory. *Of Eve.*

I refocused on myself. On the differences from the memory. Unlike before, when Eunora had brought a book to entertain herself, all I had with me was Noir, my creation. A thought struck me as I placed the bunny down next to me, propped up in a similar position as myself. I had wondered initially if objects created by [Weave of

Darkness] qualified for [Shadow Animation]. Now I could test it.

"You are made of Darkness," I whispered, "Perhaps I can give you something to do."

I felt the ice of mana flood my veins in anticipation. With a single finger, I tapped Noir's body.

"[Shadow Animation]"

Black miasma sprung from the tip of my finger, beginning by seeping out of the pad of my skin before migrating outwards towards Noir's chest and occupying the space between us. I felt the Skill telling me it required more. That I had to make a choice. And I already knew what it would be.

Infusion.

At my Willed command, the miasma dove into Noir — like an eldritch horror sinking into the bunny's body. The knit bunny twitched and jerked, an arm shooting out and a leg shifting –even Noir's head bobbed. And then it stilled for a breath before Noir leaned forward, tilting its head to look at me. Again, I felt my Skill tell me I was not yet finished. There was more to do if I wanted to animate Noir fully.

"Hello, Noir," I whispered, reaching out my hand and pulsing my Will, "*Come to me.*"

As the ice of mana filled my mouth and forced its way into my words, Noir stood in the way a puppet might stand. It stood with harsh jolts and overextended with every movement, producing an uncanny feeling that perhaps Noir truly could be alive. Or half-alive, the movements unnatural enough to create an uneasy feeling. Having finally gotten close enough, Noir held out a single knit arm to my hand before its legs went into overdrive and it stumbled. Noir continued moving towards me, unsteady on its stuffed legs, until the bunny rammed into my side and squeezed. Its soft arms pressed into my stomach, and though it was clearly using all its might, it felt like a feathered touch. Gently, I pulled Noir off of me and placed the bunny back on the table, wondering what else it could do.

As I brought my hands back to myself, I felt a weight on my wrist. Noir had wrapped his arms around me again.

I gave a small smile, "Good bunny. You can stop now."

Only, I couldn't feel the ice of mana filling my voice. And Noir did not let go.

"Noir, stop," I was firm when I spoke and pushed the whole of my Will into the command.

It did nothing. Well, not nothing. It had distracted me while Noir began running towards my stomach once more, clutching me with all the strength his little body could muster.

"Wait, no-" I pulled him off me again, holding the bunny in front of me by its stomach.

His arms and legs kicked out toward me in a hugging motion. *Come to me.* That didn't require physical contact, did it? No, a reasonable person would think it meant standing nearby. But Noir isn't a person.

Gently releasing him on the table, I was immediately gripped by the knitted bunny. I wondered what other commands I could give. How careful would I have to be with my words? It seems I only got one chance to get it right.

"Noir, this is going to be a pain," as I spoke I ran my nails along the bunny's back.

It seems I will simply have to wait out the time limit. Ten minutes of Noir's hugs —less now. It felt odd, not warm like the tight hugs from my loved ones in *elsewhere,* but I felt pleased. I had created Noir, and whatever drove my command I had not intended for it to be such a sweet action. That meant something else chose it. Maybe it was another divine machination, but something in my Skill told me that was not the case. I had given Noir life, not a God.

As I sat, I decided I might as well practice my control.

"[Shadow Manipulation+Shadow Conjuration]"

Eventually, I would not have to speak my Skills aloud. The more I used them, the less I needed the Skill names to focus my mana. But I was not there yet. Rather than unfurling the entirety of my power, I felt mana condense in the palm of my hand and disperse into the air. Silently, a growing sphere of darkness manifested into my hand.

I focused my eyes on how the sphere's surface rolled as it expanded to the size of a tennis ball, lumpy and uneven as it stopped growing. I needed to be able to shape it more precisely, like *before*. Weapons of solid shadow cut just as fiercely as weapons of steel. I just need to get to that point again.

I could feel it, my Skill speaking to me. A whisper of guidance. I can control it as expertly as before –it will just take mana and focus.

Keeping my eyes on the malformed sphere, I brought my other hand over and began physically tracking every ridge and roll, every lump and bump. And then I pushed them down, Willing them to smooth at my movements. Slowly,

I worked over the sphere, holding in my mind the idea of a smooth surface. It didn't just snap into place, no. As my fingers ran along the surfaces, I could feel my fingertips chill with mana and could see the surface collapse and expand with my touch. It wasn't until I felt Noir go limp against my side that I realized I was finished. I had kept smoothing, rolling, and condensing for the entirety of Noir's animation. And the previously tennis ball-sized shadow was now slightly larger than a ping-pong ball and was as smooth as steel.

Repositioning myself, I pushed my Will and pulled the shadow marble through the air. It swung back and forth before me, slowly drifting at my command. It took all of my focus to maintain the smooth surface as it moved, and I felt my breath catch at the realization that it was only my focus that was strained.

My mana was still full, and my Will had plenty of power to shape it.

Determined, I pulled my hands away, leaning back onto them, still staring at the floating sphere —willing it to hover directly in front of me and to float in place.

A single point, I thought to myself and to the shadow, *extend a single point.*

The marble continued to float, unmoving. Unchanged.

I took a deep breath, centering myself. I closed my eyes. I needed this. I needed to prove to myself that I wouldn't stay weak forever. That this world wouldn't ruin me. That my strength in *elsewhere* was real –not some figment of my imagination. And that I would not be trapped by the confines of the Dawn name.

A single point extended. Sharpened. A cone of darkness. No longer a sphere. A single point.

118

This time, when I opened my eyes, I was greeted with a success –though not in the way I expected. No longer was it a sphere; instead, it was an elongated cone. While it did have the sharpened point, rather than remaining rounded the end had flattened. It was a 'cone of darkness.' I huffed.

"Of course, you listened to the bit that mentioned you particularly."

Despite my disgruntled voice, I felt a small smile form. I had done it. It was small, easily fitting into the palm of my hand, but it was a start. I grabbed it from the air and held it tightly. This was what I had. This was my lifeline to something better than Eve's torment, Raphael's distaste, and Theo's apathy. It was something to keep me safe both in the Borderlands and on the perilous journey to get there.

At the thought, I felt something rough snake through my gut. Anxiety, this time all of my own. In *elsewhere* the Dome protected us from monsters –here there was no such thing. Sure, there were wards, adventurers, and heroes, but they were stop gaps for individual protections. They were not for the masses –and I could not count on them for myself. I came from a world where science and magic coexisted, where protection had long been found. This world, with its cruel Gods and free-roaming monsters, was a wasteland. Despite the beauty of this estate, I was disgusted by its very existence.

[Congratulations! Shadow Manipulation is now Level 3! Class experience applied!]

I stared at the verdant green screen before me blankly. Already? I did notice that [Shadow Conjuration] did not receive a level. *Perhaps*, I thought to myself, *Conjuration doesn't care about how it moves. Just that I've summoned shadow to me and sustained it.*

"[Shadow Conjuration]"

As I spoke, I envisioned the same cone of darkness. In dozens of spots around me, wisps of shadows materialized and grew –warping into the desired shape as I focused and forced my Will onto them. It was easier now that I knew I was just as capable as always. No, in this sense, I was even more capable. In *elsewhere* magic was but a small part of life —in Maeve and the greater Gargantua the magic of the system *was* life. To be capable at this is to be the crème de la crème. These Skills are attached to a [Rare] class for a reason.

Yet still, as I looked over the shadows that surrounded me like a locust swarm, the victory tasted bitter and I felt something horrible wrench my gut.

This victory had come at the cost of my life, after all.

I would rather be capable back *home* than spend any more time stuck in this hellish life.

Chapter Twelve

Dreya's Eyes Shine

Peak of Autumn, Week 4, Day 5

Alas, I was stuck here.

Gritting my teeth and pushing down the waves of anger that were once again boiling beneath my skin, I went back to conjuring more and more shadow cones. They were no larger than my palm, with the base still roughly ping pong ball sized and the point extended only two inches out, but the sheer number was getting overwhelming. My focus wasn't enough to keep them levitating and maintain their shapes, so they began dropping out of the air as soon as they were conjured. First, there were a dozen, then easier was a dozen more, then three dozen appeared already shaped. Soon, the cones were dripping with soft thuds to the ground —and when the ground became filled with the scattered cones, they began to pile upon each other.

Nothing had said the Skills were anything but toggled on and off, and I brought my Will to bear under that assumption. So long as the faucet was running, I produced more waves of shadow cones. The ice of mana leaving me was a constant throb, not quite painful but not quite comfortable. It was a type of manic focus I had found myself in, I was in such a frenzy to produce that I hardly did more than snap my mental image in place before creating another. Initially I had thought I would need to focus on each cone to maintain it, but once I had focused on the first dozen it became a form of blueprint that I impressed upon the Shadows.

Warmth surged from within me as I began orchestrating new piles of shadow cones, ever more until a there were six heaping mounds surrounding the table I was perched on.

I don't know how long I spent in that fugue state, focused solely on producing the cones, but by the time I found myself I was panting and a headache had begun to form at the base of my skull. The dull throb pulled me out of my focus and brought me back to the clearing, where I was surrounded by the cones.

I felt a sharp pang in my heart as I looked around at the darkness at my feet, piled high halfway to the table. It was exactly what I had pictured—crisper even than in *elsewhere*. I created another one of the cones and rolled it in my hand. The shadow made solid still produced wisps of darkness, but the core of the cone was opaque. I pressed a finger to the pointed end of the cone. The tip was sharp as a tack. I was sure, had it not been for my increased Vitality and Endurance, that I would have drawn blood. Feeling inside of myself, I felt [Quick Calculation] aid me as I attempted to judge my limits.

And it told me I could fill this clearing up past the table. And even then, I would be able to hold out and maintain them for hours. My limits were no longer the same as before —the small amount of magic that I had access to in *elsewhere* paled in comparison to the well within me now. The boon of wielding a [Rare] Class was incomparable to the instruction I'd had in *elsewhere*. Yes, the mental imaging had helped —still helped even now, as I stood and stared at the product of my focused frenzy— but without the increased Magic and Divinity within my body I would never have reached even this meager amount of progress.

I felt something akin to pride and resentment as I looked over the clearing, still gripping the cone in my hand. And

I wondered if this mattered. If being able to do all this would amount to anything.

The answer was whispered to me by the warmth I had felt while succumbing to my conjuration.

The answer was, undoubtedly, *yes.*

It means something. It has to mean something. I want that warmth again —even if part of me wants to stay cold.

The thoughts bubbled to the surface, surprising me. My heart was aching, even now, and my anger still raged on, but, even if this was a trick by the Divine, I couldn't ignore how the shadows brought me relief from the pain my loss had caused.

My eyes were dry and only a touch of the bitterness from earlier remained. The warmth hadn't left me, even as I shoved dark thoughts into my own head. It was nice in a way I had not allowed myself to feel before now. The comfort of the dark had caused me to panic before, but maybe I had just needed time to adjust to the soothing presence darkness could be.

Honestly, I never had to be without it.

With a single breath, the shadowed cones that filled the clearing dispersed into puffs of dark wisps that melded into the natural shadows of the clearing —causing them to pulse a darker shade of gray before returning to their original overcast tone.

All that remained was the single cone in my hand. It was all I needed. Between it and Noir, I had my everything.

So I leaned back and gazed up at the sky. The blue extended in all directions, not a cloud in sight. And I squinted my eyes at the two Suns well past noon. The First Sun, Troya, hung lower than the Second Sun, Dreya, due to the time of day. Troya was larger than Dreya and glowed with a ring of red light —however Dreya's yellow light was far more powerful and overtook Troya's sunlight with it's own. It was a tragic tale that made it so, not science or magic. This was caused by the Divine. In fact, I felt a memory come forward. A relatively nice memory by Eunora's standards. She loved the myths of creation, and this was no different. I let the knowledge wash over me. The myth was something I both *knew* and knew.

Dreya was said to have once been a goddess with hair like golden flax and eyes as beautiful as Troya's sunrise, though her domain has long been lost to time. Dreya had wanted nothing more than to be so beautiful as Troya's light. So she begged her beloved, Druigr, God of Dreams, to fulfill her wish. Druigr knew only one way to do so and told Dreya as such. That all he could do was allow her to sleep —and within her dreams she could become Troya and her beauty would shine upon the whole world but it would not be true. It would not be *real,* for Druigr held no sway over the sun's light.

Only later, after Dreya had thanked Druigr with her whole heart, had he realized the mistake he made.

For there was another who held power over Troya's beauty —and his name was Primus and he was the God of Light. For eons, Primus had allowed Troya to burn red and beautiful, casting Gargantua in a rosy light, and Dreya went to him and she praised Troya's beauty. Primus preened at the compliment and found himself drawn to Dreya's beauty himself. And so when Dreya asked to have some of Troya's beauty, Primus said, "If you will give yourself to me, I will give you a sliver of Troya's heart —so you may shine as bright as Troya in all that you do."

Dreya, long betrothed to Druigr, said, "I can give you anything but myself, for I have given that to another. I will give you the shade of coral I so love —or the smell of winter winds. I will give you the fire from my hearth or the golden locks of my hair."

Heartbroken, Primus cried, "I will take your eyes —for they are like Troya's sunrise. And in exchange I will give you what you so desire."

And Dreya cried out of excitement—for what are a pair of eyes to a Goddess? She can regrow them a dozen times over. And so, using a dagger made up of the summer breeze, Dreya cut her eyes out and gave them to Primus.

In exchange, Primus plucked a piece of Troya from the sky and told Dreya, "Eat and you shall be eternally as beautiful as Troya. Eat and your heart's desire will be granted."

And as Dreya devoured the heat of the sun, Primus smiled a cruel and hateful thing. For Primus was going to have Dreya in whatever form he could —just as he had made Troya his forever. Dreya was consumed by the heat of the red star, and Primus melded her into a second sun. The Second Sun.

Hours later, Druigr, recognizing the warmth from the yellow sun as the warmth of his lover, screamed with such rage the skies shook with his anger. In his rage, Druigr released the whole of his Divine might into the world. It was not long after that Primus fell into an eternal slumber.

There was no proof the God of Dreams had done anything, other than tear the mortal world asunder, not even when his tears flew into the sky and empowered Dreya's light and his ability to send Dreams dried up. Not when Dreya grew to outshine Troya and Primus still remained asleep. None could prove it taxed him so to force Primus asleep.

And so Druigr's love was reknowned amongst the remaining Gods and Goddesses and he became the God of the Second Sun while Primus became the God of the Sleeping Sun.

It was a tragedy, and Eunora had loved reading it. And I was certain that was the sanitized version. Even now, eons after the legend, Druigr was to be the one to pray to for vengeance for a lover wronged. Though she wasn't supposed to know this, Eunora had overheard that priests of Druigr mutilated rapists behind the eyes of the law — Eunora of then had not really known what that meant, but I did. And I approved. But there was a bit that had always made her wonder. What had Primus wanted with Dreya's eyes?

Perhaps I will find a better version of the story and read it on the way to the borderlands. Maybe I can bring Eunora some closure —and myself some entertainment. I had not picked up a book in months. I had not learned *more* about this world.

I squeezed the shadowed cone I still held. No longer was there time to grieve. Now was the time to grow. And so, I flicked my eyes to to where a green screen was hovering with white letters.

[Congratulations! Shadow Conjuration is now Level 3! Class experience applied!]

I felt the depth of my ability increase at once, and, curiously, it felt as if my Will was crystallizing ever stronger. *That* had not happened in *elsewhere*. In fact, it made this whole System irritating in a new way. Will was, in *elsewhere,* one's capacity for discipline and control over their magic. The fact that a Skill level could increase it was almost insulting.

Releasing my grip, I let out a breath. This was not helpful.

"I am just…" I took in the bright suns and vibrant blue sky, the fallen leaves at the edge of the clearing, the cool breeze and the cold stone I sat upon, the warm tingle of the suns on my skin, "Tired. And tired of being tired."

I sat like that, leaned back and staring up, Noir placed gently against my side, rolling a shadowed cone between my fingers, until my eyes began to water. Not in the hard way that staring at a screen had caused my eyes to well, but in the soft way right before a nap. And so I closed my eyes and leaned all the way back down spreading my arms out and dangling my legs over the edge of the table. And I napped in the warmth of the suns.

When I awoke, the two Suns were closer to the horizon. My muscles were tight as I shifted on the stone, and as I began stretching out comfortably I heard the rustle of leaves and an indignant huff. I was suddenly very aware that the shadow cone had dissipated —my ability to consciously feed it mana a requirement that was no longer met— and I quickly sat up.

"Nora, Nora, Nora," Came a sharp voice, high-pitched and filled with disgust, "Have some dignity."

I knew who this was. She haunted Eunora's memories like a poltergeist disguised as a benevolent spirit.

Evelyn. Eve. The oldest daughter of the Dawn.

Divine Tales One

The Forging of the Second Sun

Time Immemorial

Druigr, God of the Second Sun, Lord of Righteous Anger, was not always so. As with all elder Gods, his Domain has expanded, shrunk, shifted, and expanded once more. Midway in his reign in the Divine, he was the God of Dreams, Rightful Regent of Eternal Slumber. And he was betrothed to an ethereal Goddess with hair of golden flax and eyes that matched the crimson of a setting sun. So far back was it that there only hung the red sun —Troya. The Goddess's name was Dreya, and Druigr loved her more than any dream he had forged.

Such was his love that he would spin Dreya's fantasies into her mind's eye. From frolicking in a meadow of mystical flowers to fighting the fiercest beast, he would allow her to live her dreams every time she shut her eyes. There was a single dream Druigr could not give to Dreya. He could not grant her desire to be as beautiful as Troya's light, rosy and soft. Dreya was enamored with the sun's rays. She claimed they warmed her soul and brought her new life. Druigr had attempted, once, to give her what she sought. He wove a tapestry of dreams, giving her golden hair a tinge of copper and her soft skin the rosy shade of Troya's light. Her eyes became every shade sunset could bring, and her mouth a vermillion so vibrant Druigr wished it was real so he could lay a kiss upon it. He forged that dream for seven days and seven nights before he gave it to Dreya, hoping it would satisfy her. And oh, how Dreya had *loved* that dream. She loved it so much that she slept for the entire season of spring. Even then, Dreya had fought waking with all her might.

When she opened her eyes and saw Druigr's stricken face, her expression crumpled, and she dove for his feet.

"Oh, my beloved!" Dreya wailed, "Send me back, please. Make me as beautiful as our red star. I beg of you! Druigr, God of Dreams, Rightful Regent of Eternal Slumber — send me back."

With a haunted look, Druigr began to understand Dreya's illness. Her inability to see how her own beauty caused her to shine.

"My love, I cannot give you what you seek. My powers are but an imitation of life —even Primus himself would struggle to grant your wish." Druigr mourned what he could not give Dreya, and so he maligned himself, "My dreams are not truth. They could never compare to reality. I hold no control over the sun's light or its hues."

Dreya pulled herself up from Druigr's feet, ceasing her begging. She had heard him, after all. And so Dreya wrapped her arms around Druigr and laid a kiss upon each cheek, "Thank you, thank you! I won't forget this."

In his confusion at these turn of events, Druigr simply stood as Dreya showered him in gentle kisses. It took him far too long before he realized something had gone awry. And by then Dreya had long laid the final kiss across his cheek and left Druigr's presence. *Thank you,* she had said. But all Druigr had said was that he paled in Troya's light —that not even Primus, God of Light, Lord of the Forge, could wave his hand and give her what she desired.

Oh. But Druigr hadn't said that at all, had he? He had said Primus would struggle, not that he would fail.

Primus was less of a man by virtue of being a God. With bulging muscles and a harsh look, he oversaw the Divine Forge that consumed Troya's flames. At dawn he would collect her cool tones and prepare jewelry fit for a Goddess. At dusk he would take her raging crimson light and forge weaponry fit for a God. It was by his might that Troya burned so beautifully. It was by his skill that Troya shone in her rosy hues. Such had been the way for millennia upon millennia, civilizations had risen, crumbled, and risen again in the time that he had been crafting Troya's light. Long before Druigr was born of the summer storms, or Dreya was grown from golden wheat. Before Mera had slain her father, before the twins of Order and Chaos overtook Hinez's domain, such was the power of Primus, first of his name, that he could keep his power without fail.

It was a hot summer day when the golden goddess Dreya brightened Primus' forge. Her smile was gentle and her dress flowed freely with the wind. Her sandals were made of molten gold and her eyes were a rich crimson that matched Troya's deepest dusk.

Primus was enchanted so thoroughly he did not hear her praises for Troya. He needed no flattery to be drawn to Dreya, to allow her wishes to become his own. Yet still, once he found himself, he basked in Dreya's praises for the rest of the day. It was nighttime when, finally, Dreya asked if Primus could help her become as beautiful as Troya's light. If he could help her go from golden to vermillion with his power over Light.

Primus, leaning in close to Dreya, so close he could smell the fresh scent of dew on her skin, said, "I will give you your heart's desire. I will forge you into a Goddess so beautiful even my star pales."

His voice was husky and Dreya found herself leaning towards his voice —before blinking and coming back to herself.

"Will you, truly?" She smiled, ethereal and Divine, as her warmth spread to the world around her.

"I will," he nodded, running a finger across Dreya's cheek, "But you must give yourself to me. You must allow me to re-forge you as my own and only then can I give you a piece of Troya's heart. Once you do that, you will shine as bright as Troya in all that you do."

Taking a step away from Primus, Dreya's face crumpled, tears of crystal pricking her eyes, "I cannot give you myself, for my heart and soul belong to Druigr. But I will give you anything else you should want."

Primus, rage filling his belly, nearly spat, "There is nothing I desire but you. Do you not want to shine with Troya's light?"

"Oh, how I crave such a thing!" Dreya cried, "I can give you the crisp taste of winter winds —or the shade of coral I grew from my blood, with its soft pink hue! I will sacrifice the indigo flames of my hearth or the flax of my hair!"

"I crave none of this —for all I desire is *you.* Is your dream worth so little? Can you not give me a single night?" Primus put on a false face and pleaded with Dreya, falling to his knees and gripping her thighs, "One night and all you desire shall be yours."

"No -No! My dream is my everything, but I cannot betray Druigr! He is my heart and soul, as I am his!"

But Primus, close as he was to Dreya, cried into her stomach, "Oh but I could be that for you. I could be your *everything.*"

And Dreya wept at the knowledge she would never sway Primus. Then she wept because Primus was gripping her viciously now. His fingers dug into her rib cage and his body pressed into her. She wept and begged and still Primus did not release her. Not until the morning sun broke the sky.

"Now," Primus hissed, anger and hate and lust still in his voice, even after taking what he wanted, "I will take from you once more."

But Dreya was broken, unable to weep any longer, and she no longer had it in her to respond. So, as Primus reach up to her face she did not flinch. And when her eyes were plucked from her head she did not scream.

"For having the audacity to look like Troya as you reject me for another, I will send these to your lover. And I will share with him memories of our night. And never again will you be his heart and soul."

The grin on Primus was a cruel thing, an act of malice in itself. But Primus got what he wanted —Dreya found it in herself to weep again. While Primus wrapped her eyes like a present, bow and all, Dreya summoned a dagger made up of the summer breeze. But the summer breeze was meant to be gentle and kind, so the dagger was a malformed thing with jagged edges and a hilt of lush green leaves that rustled with the force of her grip.

Primus was filling the box with memories of Dreya's flesh when he heard a gentle rush of water behind him. He paid it no mind and he sent his delivery off with a ray of light. When he turned around to face Dreya once again, he screamed in horror and rage.

"How dare you, you pathetic excuse for a Goddess," he growled, pulling fire from his forge as he rushed to Dreya's collapsed form.

Her golden blood was pooling from a wound on her throat, and her head laid in a pillow of the same lush leaves from earlier. Life was draining from her and Primus roared once again.

Primus would not lose Dreya, like he refused to lose Troya eons before. Primus was not so weak as to give up without a fight, and so he channeled his Divine Might into the red flames in his palms and gave it more of Troya's light. And then he shoved the ball of flame into the socket of what had once been Dreya's right eye.

"Become consumed by me, Dreya," Primus hissed, "Orbit me like I'm your world. I will grant your heart's desire, you sorry Goddess."

Reaching up, Primus plucked a piece of Troya out of the sky and slid it into Dreya's left eye socket. As Dreya absorbed the heat of the sun, Primus began to laugh. Primus was going to have Dreya in whatever form he could. He had won, once again.

As Dreya's golden body erupted in yellow flames, Primus began to forge. First he melded her arms in flames golden as her hair, then he forced her legs to become round, and finally he tucked her head into her body. And then, once she was the shape of a small star, he threw her into the sky and placed her below Troya and a little to the left.

Dreya became a second sun. The Second Sun. And she was as beautiful as Troya. Together they gave off an orange light that cast the world in perpetual sunrise.

Druigr looked up at the sky, with its two suns, and worried over Dreya's departure. She had not returned to him. It was as that thought struck him that a ray of light deposited in front of him a golden box with a bow of clouds. Curiosity overcome Druigr and he ripped into it, thinking it a gift of thanks from Dreya after her hasty departure.

As he pulled the top open Druigr felt a rush of memories whirl through him. Memories that turned his stomach and filled him with rage. Not, as Primus had wanted, towards Dreya.

Immediately, Druigr looked to the Second Sun and *knew*. He knew it was her. His love. His heart and soul. And he wept tears of rage and grief. Then he *moved*. For Druigr was not always the God of Dreams. When he was born from the raging storms of Yrua and Orpal, lightning was in his blood. And the lightning brought with it rage and anger so visceral he could feel the electricity in his veins.

Without abandon, Druigr launched himself through the sky. No longer was his body of flesh and blood, now he was a storm cloud rolling through the sky, lightning raining down on the mortal world below. This became known as the Folly of Primus, but at the time, it was called Druigr's Rampage. No mortal land was spared in his anger and many perished at the will of his Divine Might.

It was mere hours later when Druigr had crossed the World Barrier and found Primus sitting atop his forge, staring up at the dual suns. There were no words exchanged when Druigr laid eyes upon him, no taunts or questions, simply violence.

Lightning rendered the earth beneath their feet unsteady, and thunder shook the forge Primus sat atop. Flames erupted from the forges pipes at the beck and call of Primus. Then the fight truly began. Trees were ripped from the earth, flung across the Word Barrier and knocking chunks out of mountains. Lakes boiled and burned the nymphs living within, leaving husks of the women behind.

But Primus had just forged a new sun, and he was not as young as he had once been. And Druigr was in his prime and filled with an all consuming rage.

Even still, Druigr knew he could not kill Primus. But he could wound him. And so, with fingers laced in lightning, Druigr waited until Primus flagged just enough —that was it. The moment when Primus looked to the left when he should have looked right, and stumbled. That was when Druigr ripped out Primus' eyes. They were a shining gold, just like Dreya's hair had once been.

Druigr was not a smith, not in the way Primus was. But he *could* forge and weave eternal dreams. Dreams of the future and the past. Dreams of love and hate. Dreams of heaven and hell.

Crushing Primus' eyes would have felt hollow, Druigr knew. So, while Primus clutched at his empty eye sockets, gushing the golden blood of a Divine, Druigr began to craft a dream. It was an ugly thing, of suffering and damnation and hate, but it fit Primus well. Druigr brought himself close to Primus, so close he could smell the strain of his Divine Might, could feel the tension in his body, and he filled Primus with a dream so horrible he would never wake.

Watching Primus collapse into a heap filled Druigr with a new kind of rage. A righteous anger pooled in his gut. Druigr had done no wrong, not when he rid the world of such a God. And all the heavens turned away as Druigr set to work ensuring Primus would never wake.

First, he laid him upon his bed, dropping him roughly — for he deserved not consideration. Druigr used the remnants of the summer breeze to sew Primus's eyes shut. It would not do to be caught because of missing eyes. Using Primus's own forge, Druigr wove a tapestry of power unlike even his most tangible of dreams, and he fed it the stolen eyes of the God of Light. With a burst of embers, the tapestry flew into the sky and headed for Dreya's light.

It would fuel Dreya's final dream and then some. Her dream to be as beautiful as Troya's light was foolish when Dreya had always been twice as captivating. So, sacrificing his domain of dreams, Druigr empowered Dreya and gave her all the Light that Primus had to give.

He wouldn't be needing it in his slumber.

Dreya's golden light grew to overcome the rosy hues of Troya, overpowering the original sun and casting the mortal and Divine realms in yellow light for the first time.

And so Druigr was reborn.

With a body made of the same golden tones of his beloved, he became the God of the Second Sun, Lord of Righteous Anger.

Chapter Thirteen

Eve of Change

Peak of Autumn, Week 4, Day 5

Evelyn did not look like Eunora —her clothes were too meticulously pressed, and her eyes were too sharp. Evelyn did not look like Raphael —her countenance too composed, her body language too controlled. Every part of her was prim, every wave of her hand proper. She didn't look like Theodore either. Her expression was anything but blank —the distaste from her voice clear on her face in all the subtle ways a lady was meant to show such things. The twitch of her upper lip, the slight arch of her eyebrow, the angle of her head. Subtle but not blank. She didn't look like the Countess either, though she likely would to the Eunora of before. Evelyn simply didn't hold the pressure of their mother. Unlike the others, and myself, Evelyn's hair was smooth and straight — forcefully done so that she could look ever more refined.

She looked every bit the graceful lady she was training to be. It irritated me that she actually *would* know if I was dignified. Not that it mattered here in this empty courtyard. Correction —the courtyard that was *supposed* to be empty. In fact, a courtyard so out of the way it is almost always empty.

Ah. She came looking. I felt a brow twitch in irritation. Eunora of the *before* was coursing with anticipation, worry, fear, and hope. I had to kick those feelings down for my own distaste to come up. Evelyn and I agreed on one thing —this was not a sisterly relationship. Evelyn was hateful and cruel. And Eunora loved her in the way only a younger sister could, with admiration and adoration, both in spite of and because of the harsh treatment. It was a sick sort of love fueled by Evelyn's distaste, which turned it into a need for her acceptance. Though for the Eunora of before, that was rather the trend. The worse the Dawns treated her, the more she craved their affection —and the more she wanted it, the further away it became.

Evelyn was the second oldest at 14, but even as a child she was always hateful. That had gotten worse over the years, not better.

"Well? Get off that wretched table." She hissed, stepping toward me and further into the courtyard.

I had already sat up, and my legs were nearly touching the ground, but the hurt from Eunora was fueling my irritation. So, instead of listening, I laid back down.

"Pass."

I closed my eyes and tried to keep my anger under control. It was unlike in *elsewhere*, where I had been free to express whatever I needed. Here, if I gave in to my rage, I knew I would lose whatever minuscule control I had found. And this was all I had —power over myself. Not to mention that my rage often choked me anyway, so I never fully got out the anger.

I was looking back up to the sky when I felt a breeze tickle my nose. It itched, so I turned my head —only for a streak of light to cross through where my face had just been. I snapped back up and looked at Evelyn. She still had her hand pointed toward me, and the runes circling her had yet to fade. Unlike my Class, hers clearly didn't give her a manipulation ability. The runes circling her meant she had to channel mana to move it —but the fact that she'd only manifested a bolt of light meant she had yet to contract an elemental.

"I said get up, Nora," Evelyn's smile was sadistic, and she clearly expected me to cower.

Another bubble of rage joined the others. *What is the matter with this family? Do they never rest?* And then came another thought, *They can't all think that they deserve to know my Class. This is the third time in as many days.*

I closed my eyes and let out a harsh breath, "What do you want?"

Her smile widened.

"Oh, you know, just the usual," her face and tone dropped, "Tell me what you picked. Raphael, the brute, wouldn't share -even though we *all* know you told him."

Oh, do they? I grit my teeth. They all think I am weak, something to discard at will. It is what they have always thought, no matter who occupied this body. Both souls were enraged now, and it was causing my stomach to sink. I flexed my hand to distract myself. Raphael was an idiot, yeah, and ignoring him would work. He simply got angry and stomped off. Theodore only dropped by out of curiosity. Ignoring him was an easy answer as well. But Evelyn was a different story. Ignoring her meant getting magic bolts thrown at me, or magelights to blind me, or salt in my water.

The rage in me told me *attack*. It told me that the only answer to force was force. Whatever cunning Evelyn thought she had was lesser in comparison to the power of my Class. But there was another voice, too —one that said it would make it worse. That hurting her would hurt me more. That I didn't have enough power to protect myself for long. And that voice was horrifically correct.

But still.

"Hey, are you *listening to me?*" Evelyn snapped as my eyes fell away from her and back up toward the sky.

I decided I would give it one more shot.

My eyes focused back on Evelyn as a whole, and I brought my intentions to bear. With every syllable, I infused my Will into 'engage.'

"[Sophism]"

"What? Was that a Skill?"

And as Evelyn gave a confused huff, the world came alive with red light. Strands of glowing red flowed from me, looping their way across the courtyard to Evelyn. They crawled up her legs, wrapping around her until I could barely see her sneer. It was hilarious, really. To know so assuredly I would be playing into Grel's hands. Chaos. Any way I went about it would not be like *her*. Eunora would swallow her pain and hope for the best. She would apologize or give up the information. She would do whatever Evelyn said —even to her own detriment.

I had known we were different, Eunora and I. But I was here. Living in her body. Stealing her future. Overwriting her personality with every move. And I had known Eunora was still inside me —I had inherited her memories, after all. I still had her body's responses. Usually, I tried not to think too hard about it. About what that made *me* — *a bodysnatcher? A wandering soul?* But in this moment, my rage died, and relief flooded through me.

Eunora —Nora— Nori. Whoever she was, she was, first and foremost, a child. Sad and alone and in desperate need of love. Well, I can't say I can love her in their stead. I don't think I have it in me. But I can hate *them*. Evelyn — Mallorica — Raphael — Theodore. I can hate them in her place. It's not what she wants, I can feel it in me, but maybe it'll prove they never deserved her anyway.

The red light of Chaos whirled for another moment before settling into the background, and I felt a smile spread across my face. A different kind of coldness filled me — unlike the cold numbness of grief or the ice of mana. This was *me*. _____ _____. This was me from *elsewhere*.

"Oh, *Eve.*" I slid off the table, the heels of my boots crunching a pile of leaves as I stood loosely holding Noir in one hand, "I bet you're a [Young Lady]. I bet you saw that [Uncommon] title and thought, 'I deserve this.'"

I stood lower than Evelyn by virtue of still being in a child's body. But as I took several slow steps towards her, I got a full view of the emotions warring across her face —confusion, recognition, *rage.*

"*Excuse you?*" She hissed, holding her hand out again, lighting it up with runes as she began whispering the words of mana and focusing her Will. All this only took her half a breath, and I felt a breeze across my shoulder.

[Sophism] hadn't ended, and my mind was still racing from it. Between that and my natural Perception, I could tell where I would be hit. So I stepped to the left and watched as another magic bolt flew by. Once was a fluke. Twice was skill. It was all thanks to my triple-digit Perception and my higher Dexterity.

I kept heading toward Evelyn, my pace barely bothered, "No need to excuse me. I'm not the one in the wrong."

I can't use my Skills, not really, I tsk'd mentally, *I'm not skilled enough to use them without speaking them.* I blinked as a thought occurred to me, and my smile — small as it had been— became sharper. *I don't need to hide the Divine. They won't know what they mean, just like [Sophism].*

"What are you going to do?" Evelyn choked out a laugh as she looked down her nose at me, "Hide in a corner and cry?"

"[Steal Nerves]"

My voice had a heavy cadence to it when I activated the Skill, and suddenly I knew why Eunora had screamed at me that this Skill was dangerous. Whereas I had been fueled by disgust before, my words lined with malice on principle, now I had the confidence as well. My breathing became measured, slow and steady, and I felt myself stand just a bit taller. In contrast, I could see the uncertainty filling Evelyn, from how her brow furrowed to the slight slump of her shoulders —even her eyes had lost some of their glare.

"What are you going to do?" I mimicked, my nose high and my shoulders back, *"Hide in a corner and cry?"*

"What're-" Evelyn caught herself as her voice wavered before taking a sharp breath and restarting, "What have you done?"

"Oh, me? Nothing, really." My mind was steel, my surety in her guilt growing by spades, it no longer mattered that Evelyn, too, was a child. I flinched at my own thought.

Something is wrong. I frowned, trying to control my mind. The closest I could get was answering Evelyn's earlier question, "It's not any of your business what my Class is. Or what my Skills are. Or even what I'm planning to do."

"Well-" She started but I was next to her, forcing myself to pass her, and I bumped into her, cutting her off.

"No." *Something is **wrong.*** My voice was hard, and my frown deepened. Still, my countenance grew strong as Evelyn's seemed to wither, "I'll be gone soon. Just leave me be for a while longer, yet."

And then I felt both Skills release at once, snapping back within me and causing me to gasp. I booked it out of the entry to the courtyard and bolted through the hedge maze before Evelyn could come back to her senses.

I was breathing heavily once I found myself back under the window to my room. But not from exertion. My breathing was shallow, and my heart was hammering in my chest.

Wrong. That was w r o n g. Whatever that Skill was, it wasn't meant for mortal use. It filled me with a sense of *right*. It was not just a matter of confidence. It made me feel higher than her, as if she was a bug to trample on my path to greatness. But I didn't want to be *great*. I just wanted to be in control.

I looked over my shoulder, trying to measure my breathing. Deep breath in, deep breath out. But all I could think of was how I stole something from Evelyn –and received *more.* Much like [Mental Fortitude], something inside of me was saying [Steal Nerves] did something different than the System had said.

I decided then that [Steal Nerves] was a last resort.

The two notifications that had been trying to force my attention didn't catch my notice until after I had calmed down and already climbed back into my room.

I allowed them in as I rolled up more of my [Weave of Darkness].

[Congratulations! Sophism is now Level 2! Divine experience logged!]

[Congratulations! Steal Nerves is now Level 2! Divine experience logged!]

Because that's not ominous, I sighed to myself.

I had checked beforehand that no one was around, but now I took in the emptiness of my room. What had once been an odd mixture of Dawn iconography and a child's room was now a pile of five wooden boxes —neatly labeled. Day clothes. Night clothes. Sentiments. Decor. Miscellaneous.

I wondered, briefly, what they'd decided was a sentiment, but ultimately I left it alone. Instead choosing to take the [Weave of Darkness] I'd just created and began a new pattern. This time, rather than a bunny or teddy bear, I decided to try a panda. I had the colors for it, after all.

Chapter Fourteen

The Oscarian Six Step

Peak of Autumn, Week 4, Day 6

"[Shadow Animation]"

I stared into Noir's iridescent eyes, watching the light catch and shift the color of the thread. I threw a small ball of yarn across the room.

"Fetch."

The knit bunny clumsily rose to its feet, wisps of shadow radiating from its body. Noir took slow steps across the room, going to the ball. Bending over and using its round paws, the bunny grasped the ball of yarn and turned back to me. Then, with what could only be described as a malicious glint in its eyes, dropped the ball of yarn and kicked it forcefully back to me. Only, a knit bunny doesn't really have muscles, and a ball of yarn is relatively light, so the ball pathetically rolled halfway to me before coming to a stop and forcing Noir to stomp back over and kick it again in order for the ball to actually make it back to me.

I sat cross-legged on the floor and picked up the ball before looking back to Noir. This was the fifth time this morning I had used [Shadow Animation] and the second time I had gotten this type of animation. The first, second, and third times had all been executed with an excitable bunny that dashed after the ball, not letting it out of its grasp until the knit bunny was back in my lap, sitting on top of me and thrusting the yarn ball into my hands. The fourth and fifth times were not done nearly as happily. That was about the two-hour mark, and I had begun getting testy myself because I knew Maria and her squad of maids would show up soon. Much like in the courtyard, the animations seemed to feed off my mood. Perhaps that is what it means for something to be made of my soul.

I glanced around. About a third of everything I owned was packed into the five boxes the maids had dragged in —noticeably, the entirety of my collection of knit items was packed into the box labeled 'sentiments'. I was both irritated and confused. Irritated that they had pulled the bags out from under my bed and confused as to why they weren't considered 'miscellaneous' or 'decor'. The answer to that was easy once I had pried open the respective boxes and found miniature tables and chairs stacked in individual boxes within the larger container. There was even a miniature couch that matched the one that had been in my sitting area. I nearly made the mistake of pulling one of the miniatures out before I had a rather obvious realization about the exact duplicates of the furniture that was missing from my room.

Which, of course, was that this *was* the furniture that was missing. Which meant these items were shrunk. Or the box is larger than it looks. Or both. Honestly, I wasn't sure —the deep blue runes that lined the box labeled 'decor' flowed so faintly and were so intermingled it was hard to tell when one ended and the next began.

It distracted me from thinking about [Steal Nerves] and [Sophism]. Both a different kind of trap set by the Gods. If I focused too much on either Skill, a disgust so intense it caused my stomach to roll filled me.

The ball of yarn hit my face, and my eyes snapped to the irritated little bunny halfway across the room as it sat down. It seems my time is up. I watched as the shadows living within the bunny fled Noir's knit body and turned into a mist that dissipated in the air.

[Congratulations! Shadow Animation is now Level 3! Class experience applied!]

After I used the Skill for the second time this morning, it had leveled to 2 —and given me another 5 minutes of time to run an animation.

"[Inspect]"

One day I would no longer need to speak my Skills aloud. That I was not there yet caused an uneasy feeling to itch under my skin. Instead of letting the dread fill me, I focused on the white words filling the green screen of the System.

[Shadow Animation: As a Young Lady of Darkness, you have summoned the unseen and commanded the world of the stalker. Now the unseen will use your soul to fuel a creation of your own shadow. Through your strength of will your shadows will begin to act of their own accord in line with your commands. No two shadow animations will be exactly the same. Additional animations unlocked upon level up. Duration increased upon level up. Cooldown decreased upon level up. Command comprehension increased upon level up.]

[Shadow Animation: 3rd Tier Skill. Immediate activation. Duration of 20 minutes. Cooldown of 9 minutes. Current animation options: Wisp, Infusion. Current level of command comprehension: simple. Current number of commands able to be issued: 1. Current number of animations on a single summon: 1. Current level [3] out of [80].]

Nothing but the duration and cooldown had changed. Staring at the screen, I mentally closed it —that, at least, was within my capabilities. My eyes flicked back to Noir, and the knit bunny slumped to the ground a dozen feet from me.

"Do you think you'll ever be permanently animated?" I asked the empty shell of a bunny, "There's an option that says how many animations I can use on a single summon. Do you think that means I can make you more complicated, or I can animate two of you?"

My voice was soft and unsure and unused to being either, so I could feel how it wavered. There was a brief moment I considered I could be going crazy. I was talking to an inanimate knit bunny. But it wasn't always so inanimate, was it? I created it with my own Skill, I infused my magic into every stitch, and every so often, it would come alive. Perhaps I should be talking to it more.

As I thought to myself, I felt [Quick Calculation] tell me it was once again time.

What kind of Noir would come alive next?

I stood and made my way over to Noir, wishing it would be a creation of excitement and whimsy. I wanted deeply for it to be a positive animation —I did not want my failure to overcome to bleed into Noir.

"[Shadow Animation]"

My voice was no longer soft as it became laced with the ice-cold weight of mana. I felt my breath chill as the cloud of magic left me and darkened. Wisps of shadow began clumping together as the cloud approached Noir, and upon contact, the wisps sank into the knit bunny.

I felt when the animation took hold, a presence making itself known in my mind. It was something I hadn't noticed the first few times I had used the Skill —it had only become more pronounced after reaching Level 2. At Level 3 it was undeniably real.

I had grown tired of fetch, though, so I tried something new.

"**Dance.**"

Maybe it will do a little jig, I mused to myself. Just something simple. To my surprise, Noir stood and held his hands out, and began stepping in a circle. I blinked. Still, the little bunny was turning in circles, its arms out.

I opened my mouth, then promptly closed it. I still only had one command, so there was nothing I could do to stop it. Then an odd look came across my face as a memory flooded into my mind. A memory of *elsewhere.*

Silver dresses flowed elegantly around dancing women, and I could feel the wind tussle my hair as I twirled. My hand was held firmly in a much larger hand, and I felt a weight on my waist. My other hand was gently lying atop the man's shoulder. I was looking into the distance, but his face blurred out of my awareness. I took a step back as he stepped forward. We were close, oh so close, and I let out a laugh.

So did he.

I blinked away the tears that were threatening to come to the surface and instead focused on the bunny doing the waltz. A small smile twitched at my lips.

"That's not a simple dance, Noir." I let out a light huff and sat next to the dancing bunny, holding out a hand and gently grasping one of Noir's paws, lightly spinning him, "You know, it took me weeks to get down the simplest waltz. We called it the Oscarian Six Step. I kept tripping over the side swing, and–"

I cut myself off and laughed a bit at the ridiculousness of explaining things to a bunny I had knitted out of shadow. In fact, it wasn't just the bunny bit that was weird. Sustained shadows were an odd thought too. And being a child. And dealing with the Dawns. A frown formed on my face as I thought about the past few days. It had been a series of misfortunes, from Raphael to being prone on the ground, from Theodore to the Countess. Getting thrown out of my own room for packing was unfortunate, too, as it forced me to see Evelyn. There were too few wins the past week -no, too few wins these past months. Yet still, I felt as if I was on solid ground for the first time. Despite falling into memories of *elsewhere* I was still sitting here with a clear mind.

The boiling rage was still there, though. Just under the skin. Every action served to distract me, but if I spent too long unoccupied, I would come back to the same thought.

Grel and Brel brought me here. The Countess and her children made it hell. I just want an out.

I spun Noir again, dipping him backward as he tried to continue on his own. My frown felt comical as I continued faux dancing with the animated bunny. It didn't have *awareness*. It was just my Will made manifest. I was to it what the Gods were to me. Inevitable.

I sat like that as the spell ran its course, sometimes frowning, sometimes smiling, sometimes on the verge of screaming. But not crying. Not falling apart. And with the stability came clarity of thought.

The villains in this house are children. They're not monsters to be vanquished. They can't be cut down, nor do I want to cut them down. The Countess simply didn't like Eunora. Didn't love her or hate her. To the Eunora of before, perhaps these people were worth her love. To me, they spurred irritation and distaste. None of this gave me any solace. None of this meant I was any less angry at the Gods for ripping me away from everything I knew. But thinking about it made living it ever so slightly tolerable. There was something to be said for curbing debilitating depression with an all-consuming rage.

I watched as Noir slumped back to the ground, and I leaned back. As I closed my eyes, I let out a slow exhale. I let myself release the swirling anger that had gathered in my gut and began uncoiling my emotions. With another slow intake of breath, I felt something click inside of me. [Quick Calculation] told me my mana was still three-quarters full.

"I am so over-leveled for these Skills," I breathed out as I opened my eyes and looked at the ceiling of my room — painted in oranges and pinks and purples with white clouds overlaid to mimic the sky at sunrise. The thin strands of light still twinkled above like a mockery of the night sky.

On a whim, I pulled up my [Status].

[Status Summary]

[Name: Eunora Dawn]

[Race: Human]

[Age: 8]

[Unallocated Stat Points: 0]

[Vitality: 55 Endurance: 28]

[Strength: 30 Dexterity: 56]

[Perception: 105 Magic: 55]

[Luck: 45 Divinity: 82]

[0th Tier Class: Child of the Gods, Level Max]

[Boon: Morloch's Blessing]

[1st Tier Class: Young Lady of Darkness, Level 12/20 (3%)]

[Skills:

0th Tier: Inspect Lv. 2, Weaving Lv. 4

1st Tier: Quick Calculation Lv. 2, Silent as a Shadow Lv.1, Weave of Darkness Lv. 4

2nd Tier: Otherworldly Lv. 1, Mental Fortitude Lv. 5, Shadow Conjuration Lv. 3, Shadow Manipulation Lv. 3

3rd Tier: Shadow Animation Lv. 3

Untiered: Tight Lips Lv. 1, Steal Nerves Lv. 2, Sophism Lv. 2

The green was a welcome sight. And irritatingly [Mental Fortitude] was the strongest of my Skills.

One day. I told myself, *One day, you will be strong enough to take care of yourself.*

Chapter Fifteen

The Return of a Hobby

Peak of Autumn, Week 4, Day 7

I debated it. I did. I thought maybe, just maybe, it was time. Time to brave the estate proper –not simply leap from a window sill and explore the same labyrinthine hedges. How much worse could it be, after all? In the hedges, I found the worst of Eunora's family. But there was too much unknown for me to be willing to overcome the anxiety of Eunora and head through the halls. My will faltered every time I considered it, and something snaked itself around my throat. Eunora herself had often been forced to attend the governess' class with the twins –and Raphael for a year before he aged out two years ago.

The more I thought about it, the more I wondered what had possessed Lina. She was the governess to every one of the Dawns –though the elder children hadn't attended her classes in years. All she taught was basic arithmetic, history, and religion. She must have known I turned eight –otherwise, she would be here, ruler in hand. In Eunora's memories, Lina was stern but fair. Like the rest of the estate, she was simply here for a paycheck. Perhaps if Eunora had been a genius like Theodore, a magical prodigy like Evelyn, or a martial prodigy like Raphael, Lina would have cared more about her schooling –instead of letting her fill her head with the fairytales of the Divine and the rose-hued history of the Dawns. Then again, Eunora isn't just the meekest of the elder children –she's also the fourth child, the second daughter. What use is someone so far removed from inheritance? No one invests in the child forgotten –not when Eunora lacked the traits that drew people in. Lina was also the one who would chaperone meals –the Count and Countess so rarely attending left it a wild occasion otherwise. Yet, not a word for months.

As I was lying staring at the ceiling, a knock resounded. I rolled over, grabbed Noir, and slid out of bed. Unlike yesterday, the maid squad had come closer to noon —and I was already dressed in a soft purple capelet with a white blouse adorned with ribbons tucked into a matching pair of lilac shorts. White stockings that went up past my knees, with embroidered flowers in the same soft purple, and I had to slide back into my soft leather shoes —the biggest oddity was how many shades of purple leather were in my closet even when a third of it was gone. My hair was already braided, so I had no need to do anything but leave. I prepared myself, and as I went to open the door, a second knock resounded.

Taking a slow breath, I pulled open the door, only to be assaulted by all three elder Dawns. Standing before me was Theodore, with his arms crossed. Raphael towering over the other two with a too-sweet smile. And Evelyn with a scowl so faint it could be written off as a dream.

"Oh, Nora," came Evelyn's smooth voice, "Good. You're here."

"It's time for lunch, sis," was Raphael's too-sweet voice.

"Father's home." It was Theodore's flat contribution.

I stared at the three of them, disbelief and suspicion filling me. I thought about just closing the door in their faces.

"So?" I pushed out.

Raphael's smile dropped, whereas Evelyn's grew. Theodore did not react.

"*So*, it's time to stop throwing a tantrum. We've got to eat together," Evelyn's voice was sharp despite her smile, and I saw Theodore shift his arms.

I felt my irritation grow, and I heard myself speak before I could bite my own tongue, "Oh, do we now? Since when? Because we haven't shared a meal since Rise."

"Well–" Theodore started, just to be cut off by Raphael.

"Come off it! Who do you think you are?" He hissed, voice low, "Stop acting out and just do as always. We're already running behind because of you."

When Raphael began reaching out to grab me, it happened quickly. I leaned back and slammed the door, only for Raphael to try and hold it open —which led to the door slamming down on his hand as he was unsurprisingly ill-prepared for the force I used. While in the grand scheme of things 30 Strength may not be much, it was certainly more than he had expected. Raphael let out an undignified yelp, and I cracked open the door to see his quickly reddening face —as well as odd looks from Evelyn and Theodore. I only had a brief second to consider what this would look like.

"You'll leave me be —and ice that hand— if you know what's good for you."

I decided I didn't care all that much about what it looked like and decided to lean into it. They were infuriating anyway. Before they could fully respond, I snapped the door closed, flipped the lock, and made my way out the window —a now familiar passage out of my room. Maria could simply unlock the door if she needs to wrap up whatever packing she wants to get done today. Or not. At this point, I really couldn't care less. And there really wasn't much left of my room after yesterday's packing frenzy. There was what remained of my closet, a vanity, an empty bookshelf, and my bed with a spare set of bedding folded up next to it.

"[Silent as a Shadow]"

The ice-cold feel of mana enveloped me as the world dulled into shades of gray. The only thing as vibrant as before was my irritation. It was festering beneath my skin, and I wanted to scream. *Evelyn* and *Raphael* and *Theodore* have no right to bother me. One day was too short a reprieve from them. So, when I arrived at one of the courtyards in the hedge maze, I did something truly sensible this time. I made sure to stay awake –and I sat in the front corner so no one could see me. No naps or sunbathing in a wide open space for me –not when the Dawns were roaming about. Perhaps in the borderlands, I would be able to relax. As I settled into the corner, I was greeted with a System notice in its evergreen hues.

[Congratulations! Silent as a Shadow is now Level 2!]

"[Inspect]"

[Silent as a Shadow: You are noticed, yet ignored. You lurk, yet no one cares. Like a shadow, your presence is taken as fact. This skill allows you to blend in plain sight. So long as you do not draw undue attention to yourself, it is harder to be found suspicious. This skill requires mana to maintain. Ability to mute your aura increased per level. Decreased relative perception per level. Duration limited. Cooldown applies.]

[Silent as a Shadow: 1st Tier Skill. Duration of 10 minutes. Cooldown of 2 hours. Current level of [2] out of [40].]

A single level had increased its duration from 5 minutes to 10. Would that continue at the same rate for 40 levels?

[Quick Calculation] told me that if that held true, then I would be able to use the Skill for over three hours at a time. But unlike my other Skills, this one did more outside its description than the rest. And it had yet to level past 2 —despite my using it multiple times. Like [Quick Calculation] and [Inspect], growing the Skill took more effort. I didn't know why, but that, too, left a foul taste in my mouth. Most of the System was supposed to be taught after Awakening —only until this week, no one even knew I had aged up.

My skin crawled at the thought of my ignorance. Anger welled in my stomach and I felt righteous indignation begin to overcome my senses, the edge of my vision darkening. My throat began to constrict—

"*No.*" I brought my hands roughly to my face, slapping my cheeks with all the force I could stand. As the stinging settled in, I choked out another, "*No.*"

I snapped my head to the side, looking at where I'd dropped Noir. My anger was fueling me. I didn't want to create another being of rage. I could barely handle myself. So I chose a different path.

"[Weave of Darkness]"

A neatly rolled ball of black yarn formed from the overcast shadows hiding me.

"[Weave of Darkness]"

Another black ball, this one with thinner, more thread like strings.

"[Weave of Darkness]"

This time a ball of iridescent yarn formed, the light striking it from all angles.

"[Weave of Darkness]"

Another iridescent ball with thinner, more thread like strings. The black was receding from the edges of my vision and my choppy breaths began to smooth. But I was a well of power.

"[Weave of Darkness] [Weave of Darkness] [Weave of Darkness] [Weave of Darkness] [Weave of Darkness]"

Balls of yarn and thread began to pile in front of me. It was the opposite of destructive and the more I spoke the more I felt the pathway the mana was making to create the materials.

I didn't stop.

"[Weave of Darkness] [Weave of Darkness] [Weave of Darkness] [Weave of Darkness] [Weave of Darkness] [Weave of Darkness] [Weave of Darkness] [Weave of Darkness] [Weave of Darkness] [Weave of Darkness]"

[Congratulations! Weave of Darkness is now Level 5! New features unlocked!]

[Weave of Darkness] [Weave of Darkness] [Weave of Darkness] [Weave of Darkness] [Weave of Darkness]

I didn't even notice that as I continued using the Skill, I had stopped speaking. Or that there was now a deep green shade mixed in with the black and iridescent balls of material.

[Weave of Darkness]

It was freeing to release my anger in a productive way. But as I used the Skill once more, I felt a snap inside of me and the ice cold of my mana refused to manifest another ball of yarn. Something told me I could keep pushing if I wanted to, but as I reached for the Skill the coldness was no longer kind. It was sharp and uncomfortable and I decided it wasn't worth it.

Looking around myself I took a breath.

"This is an eyesore." I sighed as I leaned forward, my hands draped over my knees.

"**[Quick Calculation]**"

I counted 25 hefting balls of varying colors, most were the black of a Shadowless Night, some were the iridescent of a Shadowless Day, and two were the green of what [Inspect] told me was a Shadowless Forest. I held those two reverentially, digging my fingers into the soft yarn. I had never loved a color more than the deep evergreens I could see from the Dome in *elsewhere.* They were so rare under the glass —so few trees that weren't tinged with the red hues of the doru-nutrients that fed them. Even surrounded by the hedge maze, with its dull greens and blues, the dark green of the yarn was deeper than the System notices that popped up in my head.

Suddenly, I was hit with a horrifying realization as I turned my head back to Noir, "How am I going to get these back to my room?"

The silent bunny wasn't capable of judging me. Intellectually I knew that. I huffed.

"Right, yeah, I'll try and weave a quick basket."

Taking the thickest yarn I used [Weaving] to guide me as I began twisting the yarn using my fingers and arms. I was small enough and the thick loops it would create were still tight enough they would be able to hold the balls of yarn and thread. I sat like that, looping and tucking and passing the yarn from hand to hand, for the rest of the afternoon. Thanks to my Skill and Eunora's muscle memory, I was quick as ever as I did my best to make a rucksack shape large enough to hold all 25 balls of yarn.

As the suns began to set over the horizon, the only trick left was to carry everything back up through the window. Only that wasn't possible. I wasn't able to add handles or any way to actually grip it.

Whether I was ready or not, it was time to go through the manor.

Chapter Sixteen

The Manor in Which We Find Ourselves

Peak of Autumn, Week 4, Day 7

I started by taking a breath and staring at the loosely knit bag I had made. It was half my size and filled to the brim with different-sized balls of yarn. I couldn't feel the passive aura of [Otherworldly] surrounding me, but I knew as soon as I used [Silent as a Shadow], I would be able to feel it contract. And I had ten minutes of [Silent as a Shadow]. It should be enough.

I fell into thought of Eunora —of how she would search out her siblings throughout the estate. My room was on the second floor, and if I entered the manor from the back, I would have to go through the atrium and the Aurelian Room to get to the main hallway. Then I would have to follow that to the entryway and climb the stairs. From there, it's only two corners to return to my room. Eunora knew there were passageways for the maids, but she never paid close attention to what they were, so they were hardly featured in the movie marathon that played in my dreams. So going straight through was my only option, no matter how open it left me.

Ten minutes. I would have to wait until I was out of the hedge maze to activate my Skill. And I would be carrying the sack of yarn.

Tucking Noir into the top of the bag, I patted his head.

"I could just leave all the yarn behind," I mused, "The maids would know it was me —and probably Theodore if he heard about it."

I glanced at the bag of yarn made from *my* Skill. *My* shadows. *My* mana. And I knew that would never happen. I would make something from them. [Weaving] was an odd skill, with the way it added to my actual ability to knit —increasing my speed and giving me knowledge of different styles, from knitting to crochet to hand weaving raw wool into fabric. It had been a distraction from the overwhelming pain of losing my old life. And now, it would be a way to center me through my rage.

The bag was easy to lift, not because it was light but because my Strength made such things easy —while my Dexterity allowed me to maneuver my grip as if it *did* have handles. My balance was not even off-center. My vision was limited, though, and I had to peer my head around the bulk in order to see in front of me. The dim evening light was child's play for my triple digit Perception, allowing me to catch the outline of every twitch the wind sent through the hedges and every rustle in the moongrass —both from the wind and small animals in the distance. The day's warmth was quickly seeping away, and I decided to move. Or, rather, speak.

"[Quick Calculation]"

I wasn't sure if it would work, as [Quick Calculation] had seemed to be passive —and tracking time was only *based* on counting, so there was also that. But as soon as the Skill was spoken aloud, I felt the ice of mana flood behind my eyes deep into my mind. What had once been best guesses suddenly became detailed measures of time down to the second.

It had taken me four minutes and thirty-eight seconds to reach the clearing from my room. But it had taken Eunora 7:58 to get to the atrium. And then another 9:22 to wind her way through the manor. That was just enough time from the atrium to my bedroom now that [Silent as a Shadow] has leveled to 2. There wasn't room for error.

I stood still, closing my eyes and listening deeper to the sounds of the maze. There was the same whistle of the wind shaking leaves, but the tiny thumps of animal feet became clearer as I focused. There was no laughter in the distance, no sounds of a garden cart or clanging of swords. The maze was empty. There were no fateful encounters for [Otherworldly] to draw to me, and the longer I waited, the more time there was for that to change. My eyes snapped open. It was time to go.

Eunora's memories guided me out of the maze, turns I'd never seen becoming my path as I moved one foot in front of the other, precariously balancing my makeshift bag in front of me. Only a prayer that my Dexterity would keep me nimble.

No, I hissed to myself, *No more prayers. Not in this world with Gods who would play with mortal lives. Not even to the Gods of Elsewhere.*

I grimaced at the thought but continued a steady, yet careful, pace through the hedges until a familiar fountain came into view with a familiar statue. Lyla. As I passed under an archway decorated with the same Dawn Roses I had used to offer tribute to the statue earlier in the week, the dim light of the setting suns made the courtyard appear bleak and unsettling. I decided not to linger, heading straight for the most ornate archway behind the statue —the one that led to the back entrance of the manor.

I took another pause on the other side of the archway, listening and looking for anything I wanted to avoid. I had walked into an ample open space with browning and yellow-green grass. Leading towards the towering building was a cobblestone path that turned and wound around fountains and statues. Occasionally the trail would split to lead to benches off to the sides that sat below Wilting Willows —in the daytime, the white vines that flowed down would provide just enough shade to be protected from the sunlight. Now, in the twilight hours, such shade was barely noticeable. In the distance, I heard the sounds of deep-voiced chattering and the occasional ringing of a bell—the sounds of life at the manor.

I debated activating [Silent as a Shadow] then and there, the anxiety of Eunora overwhelming me —telling me it wouldn't do to be *caught*. Not like this. *Not if we want them to love us.* I cringed at the thought and pushed it back, letting it fuel my determination—and, later, my rage. I would unpack the 'us' eventually. Probably.

Instead, I slunk off to the side of the long winding path and stepped off the cobblestones to head straight for the hedges that were cast in shadow.

I may not be able to retract [Otherworldly] or supernaturally mute my steps, but Shadow was something I could use.

"[Shadow Manipulation]"

As the coldness of mana left me and diffused into nothingness, I bore my Will and sent a single thought to the shadows that lurked in the hedges: *Cover me.* It wasn't precision work, it was quick and uneven, but the command brought the shadows around me, darkening the world surrounding me and allowing me to blend into the fringes of the path as I walked towards the atrium.

The glass dome was sparkling with the setting suns' light. Even so, I could see the iron ornaments that swirled along the glass panes that made up the atrium. Inside, I knew there would be sweeping vines, more Dawn roses, and a half dozen cafe tables ready to be set up for tea at any time. Anxiety welled within, pressure all my own —it wasn't truly about running into others. I'd seen enough of the Dawns this week for another encounter to be negligible. Still, it felt like stepping into the manor and exploring was accepting this world. If I walked through and remembered Eunora's memories, her pain, and her happiness, it would overcome me. And what if I was no longer *me?* My true name was already ripped from me, and it's hard to say this grief is who I always was, but what if I become an amalgamation of Eunora and _____? What if I come to hate that too?

That thought brought me to the door, and a whispered "[Silent as a Shadow]" dulled the world around me, leaving me to see in shades of gray. That did help to ease my anxiety as I nudged one of the towering doors open and slipped inside, the weight of [Otherworldly] shrinking. The filtered twilight was dimmer here than in the garden, diffracted through the panes of glass, and the shadows matched the swooping design of the iron ornaments. I had to move as swiftly as possible –my timer had begun to tick ever downward. I was lucky that the atrium was empty.

The problem with dulling the world is that suddenly my Perception no longer went as far. Everything was muddled, from the creaking of the ceiling to the metallic tinkling of the wind chimes. Even though I could hear them, they were no longer defined. But I didn't have time to dwell too much on it, so I powered through the atrium until I came to the Aurelian Room — already open. Usually, the doors were shut, but a thick curtain hung in the open doorway right now, and shadows flickered as the candlelight shifted within. Down the middle, I could see glimpses of maids shuffling from one side to the other, their chatter unintelligible through the shroud of [Silent as a Shadow].

It was now or never, then. Either I would get caught here, my Skill failing against their Perception, or I would be one step closer back to my room.

The answer was rather anticlimactic when I slid in between the curtains and followed the round edge of the room the short fifteen feet to the open doorway. The maids were both on the other side, dusting the mantle showing the Battle of the Golden Dawn —where the late Count Aurel demolished the Kerten forces two hundred years prior. The whole room was based on the man, with hues of gold glimmering even through the shadow surrounding me. I chose not to dwell on the sight as I entered the main hallway and past the recreation rooms — music, art, literature. There were rooms on both sides meant for such things. But I clung to the wall as I hustled past, not bothering to look within the rooms. Luckily, none seemed occupied tonight. It wasn't until I was halfway up the stairs that I noticed it was unusually quiet on the second floor. There were only three of us on that floor, true, and the twins were on the opposite wing from me. But there should still be *something*. Maids or footmen, or even a roaming guard.

As I arrived at the second floor's landing, I sped up down the hallway that would lead me back to safety. To the one place in this manor that brought me calm. To my own room. I only had three minutes left of my Skill. I needed to make it back quickly. A short while later, I rounded the first corner, then the second, and I was at thirty-three seconds. I was so close. I sped up.

I was so focused on how close I was, how I had evaded the entirety of the estate, that when I focused on my door I didn't process what I was looking at. Not immediately.

Seven seconds left. At six seconds, I paused, staring in dismay at my door. I sat down the basket of yarn, bringing my hands to my hair, tugging gently on my braids. Five seconds. I couldn't get past the door. Because a man was standing there, leaning his red-violet-clad shoulder against the wood frame. Four seconds. He was tall, the top of his head nearing the top of the hung portrait next to him. Three seconds. I knew if he were looking my way, his eyes would be a glowing blue. One second. It was coming, and there was no escape. I pulled Noir out of the basket, gripping him close to me.

[Silent as a Shadow] broke, the mana rushing back into me and the vibrancy of the manor blinding me momentarily.

He turned around. The scowl that was ingrained in my memory was present even at that moment.

"Eunora." Count Evenor Dawn spoke harshly, without love or affection. Without softening the clip of his tone. Were I truly Eunora, I would be in tears already. She often was. But though I had anxiety thrumming in my veins, I was not Eunora. Not in the same way. His coldness actually helped ease my nerves. Helped funnel my anxiety back where it belonged —to the fire in my gut. The anger.

Eunora is eight. Eight years old. What have you people been doing?

"Count Dawn."

He turned his cold blue eyes away from me and back to my doorway, stepping inside—the command to follow unstated. Despite my desire to avoid him, I used one hand to drag the bag of yarn and the other to grip Noir as if my life depended on it, and I went in after my Father.

Eunora's father? At this point, the differentiation was pointless. Eunora has been gone since the day I overtook her. Now all that remains is the vestiges of her life in me.

He did not sit down, choosing instead to go to my now empty bookshelf and scrutinize some invisible speck of dust.

"You leave the first of the week. You know this?"

Rather than respond, I continued dragging the bag of yarn to my bed. Setting down Noir, I hefted the bag on top of my duvet and let it spill out. I began sorting through them, starting by sifting the bag to get to the two green balls of yarn. I quickly slid them beneath the nearest pillow, hoping the Count had not caught sight of them. Green was, after all, not permitted in the Dawn house.

"There is a contingent of Dusk Knights headed back to Fellan. They will escort you on the journey," he continued, without a care for my response, "You will act with dignity befitting a Dawn."

Considering you and your children, that's a rather low bar. I sneered to myself. I began to separate the black and iridescent yarn from each other less discretely.

"The maids of the manor have not volunteered to accompany you, so it will be you and you alone. I've heard you've gotten rather adept at fending for yourself these past months, so that should prove to be a non-issue. You're lucky your governess has been on leave for so long. Lina would not have stood for this... *disobedience.*"

I glanced back at the Count. Sharp blue eyes met sharp blue eyes, and I fought back the disgust that welled within me. I wanted to say something venomous, something hateful, and rude. But I exercised a modicum of self-control and settled for a flat response.

"My apologies."

He gave a dry huff in response, "I'm sure. The journey will take two months. It will be by carriage, so prepare yourself. I have arranged for Maria to put together a selection of books necessary for a Dawn. Read them, or don't. Your mother has made clear to you the consequences of continued sloth."

My throat tightened, memories of Eunora all but begging this family for affection. Affection they were clearly incapable of giving. It caused something inside of me to break.

"Exile this, Dawn that, consequences, punishments, shame, disloyalty," I rolled my eyes, "Is there anything else?"

Count Evenor arched an eyebrow, but when he spoke, his voice was the same cold tone, "You mother and I know about your [Class], Eunora."

A chill crept up my spine, I had thought they assumed the same as Raphael and Theodore. Still, uncaring of the dread pooling in my stomach, he continued.

"And based on those *things* on your bed, I would say extremely specialized in Dexterity. It's [Uncommon], at least. That means you are a contender to your siblings. When the time comes, there will be expectations of you. Meet them."

I wanted to laugh. *That's it? No further thought? Just 'stop throwing a tantrum and fall in line'? No questions?*

"Your mother and I will not be seeing you off, we've been called to the Capital for urgent business. You have tomorrow to say your goodbyes, though based on your behavior I doubt anyone would want them."

The rest was a blur as he wrapped up his nonsense and left my room. I wondered, briefly, if the Dawn line was cursed. If that's what made them all so intolerable. Then I remembered Eunora of the before. Of how sweetly she treated those around her, how quiet and serious and hardworking she was, and I knew that whatever faults stemmed from this blood, they had not ruined her. And they still wouldn't if I had my way.

Chapter Seventeen

Morning Haze

Peak of Autumn, Week 4, Day 7

After the Count had left, emotion overcame me, and I grabbed a ball of yarn and chucked it at the door. And then another. And another. Until 23 out of the 25 balls of yarn found themselves violently thrown across the room with an unsatisfactory soft thud. No matter how hard I threw, the thud hardly made a sound. I needed something heavier. I whipped my head to the next heaviest object, Noir, and grabbed him with as much force as I could muster. My arm was raised, half-cocked, and ready to launch him at the door.

I paused, gritting my teeth and jerkily lowering my arm.

"**[Shadow Animation]**" I hissed, ready to tell Noir to *run* or *clean* or *hit,* ready to test the limits of what I could convey in a single word. Ready to make the bunny satisfy my rage.

Instead, I took a breath and reminded myself, "**Breathe.**"

With a shock, I felt the ice of mana leave me. Bringing my arm back down, I looked at Noir more closely, checking to see if the command had truly caused the bunny to breathe. The answer was, of course, no. There was no gentle rise and fall of the bunny's chest. I didn't feel the wind of an exhale tickle my knuckles. Instead, the soft paws of the knit animal reached out toward me, struggling gently against my grip. I brought him closer to where he seemed to be reaching for –me. My anger was stalled due to my surprise. Noir continued to reach his arms out, clearly trying to get me to bring him ever closer. His struggling didn't cease until his paw was firmly pressed against my chest. I held my breath, waiting to see what he would do. Only that seemed to be the wrong move because Noir immediately started tapping my chest with his paw. It wasn't violent, not really. It was more insistent. I took a sharp breath, and Noir turned his head up to me and tapped my chest again as I held my inhale. Seconds later, he tapped me after I exhaled.

Breathe, I repeated to myself, tearing up, "You're helping me breathe."

I wiped my eyes with my free hand and continued breathing with guidance from Noir. Slow inhale, *tap*, slow exhale, *tap,* and repeat. After several minutes I began to feel the boiling anger beneath my skin calm. I continued staring at Noir, listening to his tapping –even when it intensified as my mind drifted, wondering what this meant. Wondering if this would ever happen again. Wondering if this was truly a part of me or if I had broken off something of myself and sacrificed it to create the current Noir. I took a slow inhale, *tap,* a slow exhale, *tap,* and repeated the process.

For twenty minutes, my bunny helped me calm down. Helped me find my composure. My will. Myself. And that was what he was, really. Noir had stopped being simply a knit animal to me. He was a partner, a friend, and I could give him life at will. He was all I had in this manor that rejected me at every turn. He was solace in the dark. Noir was so much *more.* And it may have been that I was simply starved for connection that caused me to cling to him, to embrace him even after the animation ended. But in *elsewhere*, there were golems much like Noir, called by different names and serving different purposes, but they had earned the respect of the Dome. And Noir had earned that from me. Because despite being made of magic, he had taken a part of me that was alive and made it all his own. Noir had proved he was capable of shaping the command word to suit his mood, and, in my turmoil, he showed me compassion. Every time.

"I don't care if I'm projecting," I decided, holding the bunny in front of me gently, "Noir, it's you and me. You and me and this horrible house."

As the cooldown ticked ever closer to zero, I found a new goal. The more I level [Shadow Animation], the more Noir could do. The more complicated he could act, the more freedom he possessed, the longer he could be around, and the less he would sit inanimate.

"**[Shadow Animation]**"

"**Hug.**"

It was self-indulgent, but I didn't care. I had the rest of the night to contemplate what my orders would mean. And I enjoyed the feeling of Noir embracing me back. As the timer hit twenty, a green notice appeared.

[Congratulations! Shadow Animation is now Level 4! Class experience applied!]

Immediately I pulled used [Inspect].

[Shadow Animation: 3rd Tier Skill. Immediate activation. Duration of 25 minutes. Cooldown of 9 minutes. Current animation options: Wisp, Infusion. Current level of command comprehension: simple. Current number of commands able to be issued: 1. Current number of animations on a single summon: 1. Current level [4] out of [80].]

I stared at the singular change, the length of time. As soon as the cooldown hit zero, I began again.

"**[Shadow Animation]**"

"Roam."

Noir toddled around, going from me to the edges of the near-empty room and back again. He looked under the bed, in the pile of yarn, and on the lowest shelf of the bookcase before he went inanimate once again.

"[Shadow Animation]"

"Collect."

Noir rolled all 23 balls of yarn back to me, working slowly to get them stacked into a pile. It was clear that 'simple' commands were more than just the word used. They still sent meaning through whatever mana construct was connecting us. There was no other explanation for the care that Noir put into organizing the yarn.

…

"[Shadow Animation]"

"Dance."

…

"[Shadow Animation]"

"Play."

It was late into the night when Noir was rolling one of the green balls of yarn that I had tucked under the comforter back and forth. At one point, as my eyes were drooping, he began rolling one ball of yarn into the other and even attempted to stack them like building blocks —which, of course, ended in one of the balls of yarn rolling down and away on the bed.

I awoke to light from the suns filtering in through the window and the undeniable presence of the System rewarding my late night antics.

[Congratulations! Shadow Animation is now Level 5! New features unlocked! Class experience applied!]

[Shadow Animation: 3rd Tier Skill. Immediate activation. Duration of 30 minutes. Cooldown of 8 minutes. Current animation options: Wisp, Infusion, Weapon (small). Current level of command comprehension: simple. Current number of commands able to be issued: 2. Current number of animations on a single summon: 2. Current level [5] out of [80].]

I took a moment before—

"[Inspect]"

[Current animation options: Wisp, Infusion, Weapon (small)]

[Wisp: An amorphous blob of shadow with substance manifested for the sole purpose of being animated.]

[Infusion: Utilize pre-created shadow constructs and animate them based on the ability of the construct.]

[Weapon (small): Utilize small weapons no larger than 100 cm^3. Can only consist of weapons capable of being shaped at the current level of Shadow Manipulation.]

I stared at the list of animations and felt a comfort seep out of me. I had Noir –and I had another way to gain power. It was a gift to wake up to. A gift I had earned through the torture that was living in Gargantua. In Maeve. In this house.

I cleared away the System notices and rolled over to grab Noir, who had been left inanimate a mere foot from me as I had drifted to sleep.

[Shadow Animation]

I felt the power run through me as I used the Skill, a small sense of pride at the ability to use it nonverbally clenched my heart as the ice of mana flooded the air surrounding me and sank into Noir's body. With a thought, I stretched my arm over the edge of the bed and grabbed the knit panda I had been working on over the past few days. It was yet to have a name, like the other knit animals packed away. I felt my mana extend past my fingers and sink into the mix of black and iridescent yarn body.

"Follow me."

Two words this time, rather than one. The potential for more complicated sentences. Both knit animals began shifting in my hands. Sliding off the bed, I placed them both down and took a tentative step away from them before looking back over my shoulder. Both animals were toddling after me, Noir smoother than the panda. I kneeled low, waiting for them to reach me.

"Noir and–" I let thoughts of darkness and shadow fill me, a smile twitching on my face, "Haze. There, now you both have names that suit you."

I spent the morning circling my room, watching Noir and Haze track my moves and attempt to follow me. At one point, I had climbed back into the bed and waited for them to follow, only to see them both distressingly reaching up the edge of the bed frame, jumping with their short legs, unable to climb up. I promptly grabbed them both and placed them gently on the mattress to allow them to pursue their goals.

Mid-morning, I braved what was left of my closet to find a bag –of which there were somehow still half a dozen displayed, each in a different shade of purple. I grabbed a deep purple with indigo and gold embroidery. I had yet to bathe, and so I picked an outfit that matched the bag and went to get ready. Rather than braiding my hair, I left it wild –simply combing it while it was wet and waiting for it to inevitably re-coil and flow like a black mane around me. Tucking Noir and Haze into the bag, I wore it over my shoulder and took the only path I still felt comfortable using –the window.

I made my way through the hedge maze, pausing at the fork in the path –where I usually veered right to get to the clearing Eunora loved to laze in. Only, the Count had mentioned a set of knights had arrived with him –and they would be taking me to Fellan. *The borderlands.* It was the edge of the Dawn territory, bordering Calsta. It's a two-month trip to arrive by carriage, an unfathomable distance to travel in solitude.

Eunora had only ever met the knights at the manor and only in passing when they were doing rounds. There were a few whose names she had remembered, a few whose names she had forgotten, and many who she wouldn't recognize in a lineup. Perhaps now was the time to meet them, to make an impression more than a disobedient, disloyal child.

I swallowed. Eunora was scared, I could feel her fear of rejection coursing through me. It was different than the pain she had when it came to her family. This fear was more visceral, turning my stomach and causing bile to rise up my throat.

Eunora, you poor anxious child, I groaned to myself. Her anxiety was eating me alive –only that was just it. It was *hers.* These knights were charged to protect, I knew I didn't need to fear them –whether they liked me or not, though one was clearly more preferential.

I took a breath, feeling for my Skills.

"[Sophism]"

The world slowed and came awash with red light before settling into strands of pink and white. Whenever I looked down the path leading to the training grounds, the color intensified to a deep crimson.

Brel would hate what I planned to do next. Grel, unfortunately, would love it.

Chapter Eighteen

Goodbyes Are Fore Loved Ones

Peak of Autumn, Week 4, Day 8

It was easier than I thought, choking down the disgust that [Sophism] brought. It hadn't been a conscious thought, deciding to use the Skill. Not really. It was more impulse and morbid curiosity. I had known it would be a red path –just as I had known the first time I roamed the maze that it would be a white path. To know and *know* are comforting things. Even if it meant utilizing a Divine Skill from Brel.

As I walked, I gave a soft "**[Silent as a Shadow].**"

I felt the aura of [Otherworldly] contract and a weight lifted from my shoulders. The attention [Otherworldly] was destined to cause was unsettling. Under my skin, I could feel the hum of anxiety that Eunora was constantly fueling. Even that subsided with the activation of [Silent as a Shadow]. The Skill did ever more than I had expected, and it was a relief. The world dulled around me, and I continued onward. I would break the Skill once I was in the range of one of the knights, but I didn't want to tempt fate too much. So, I focused on my movements, absorbing the silence that surrounded me, letting it calm my storming emotions.

It was probably a waste of the Skill, if I was honest. I continued on, the hedges growing sparse as I continued on down the far path. No longer did the hedges turn and twist around the grounds. Now it was a straight shot to the training hall. The softness of the morning light was quickly burning away as the day grew later. It was only a few minutes of meandering before the dark stone building that housed the knights cropped up behind a copse of trees which meant there were no more hedges. This was it. The comfort of the familiar maze was washed away.

I broke [Silent as a Shadow] and felt the vibrancy of the world flood my senses. In the distance, I could hear the deep shouts of men and the clank of metal hitting metal. This was my destination. The household guards of the estate and the Dusk Knighthood are both housed here. And there was a difference. The guards stayed here perpetually, several dozen men and women that protected the manor from local, mundane threats. The guards would recognize me, and they would know the reality of the Dawns. The Dusk Knighthood was different. They were a military legion sworn to the Dawns. There were only two ways to leave the knighthood: death or disgrace. Joining was easy. It was the staying that was hard. The Dusk had a presence everywhere the Dawn reached. From the Western Border to Central Maeve, the Dusk performed rounds through every backwater town, fought monsters in every stretch of land, exerted justice on behalf of the Dawns. They are the only knights the House of Dawn uses. Which means they are who would be taking me to Fellan.

I didn't bother going through the barracks, instead circling around the side –trying not to focus too much on the emblem of the dual suns emblazoned on the stone walls. I needed to know how much more hurt Eunora would feel on this journey. Would she be rejected yet again? Would they scorn her like her own family? Would they even bother to pause and look twice at a child on the training grounds?

I took a deep breath, mentally cataloging the feel of Noir and Haze in my bag. At the worst, I would still have them.

Then I rounded the final corner, taking in the sight of a half dozen knights propped up against a wooden fence, sweat pouring from their brows as they looked over a large swath of dirt that held another half dozen knights sparring. They all looked exhausted. As I focused on a pair of men standing to the side, I noticed they weren't really men. Boys would be more appropriate. They didn't look any older than Raphael –fourteen at the least, sixteen at the most. One had vibrant red hair cut short –the other was pulling his blonde hair back in a ponytail. They must have unlocked the squire [Class]. Or maybe they were just really good. Who knows. I ran my eyes along the rest, noticing four women in the group. One was standing with the boys, towering over them. Two were on the training ground, sparring. The last was standing next to a man who made Evenor look short, with bulging muscles and a bald head. He was shouting commands at the rest of the group.

The moment I left the safety of the shade, the leaves crunching under my feet, I felt the attention of everyone in the vicinity shift to me. I could feel the anxiety of Eunora welling up within me, her fear of being *seen* hitting me like a brick. My breath caught. It was overwhelming. I shouldn't have wasted [Silent as a Shadow] on the walk over. That was stupid. I slid my hand into my bag and gripped Noir's hand, pulling him out of the bag and holding him close to me. I swallowed Eunora's fear and took another step forward. And another. Then the world stood still as the bald man appeared before me in between breaths. He had been several dozen feet away, but now he was just out of reach. And I hadn't seen him move.

He stared down at me, his mouth pressed into a firm line. I felt my pulse quicken, both my own fear mixing with Eunora's.

He hates me already! Eunora screamed within me. *This man is a m o n s t e r,* came my own voice, circling my head.

Taking hold of myself, I straightened my back. *Fear is nothing. I've been afraid. This man will not hurt me.*

"I am Nora." My voice was steady in a forced way, in a way that screamed, and I looked up and into the man's eyes. My fingers dug into Noir as I spoke.

It was a moment, no more, of silence. But I felt it stretch. And then the man nodded.

"Lady Eunora, I am Oberon Rellar, the Knight Captain of Fellan, the 43rd contingent of the Dusk Knighthood." I blinked. His voice was not soft or gentle. It was definitively rough, like gravel on a barren road, but it was not rude. It was not harsh in the way of the Countess or cold in the way of the Count. I loosened my grip on Noir ever so slightly. The eyes of the rest of the knights stopped me from relaxing my grip fully.

Sir Rellar was looking down at me —out of necessity, he was easily double my height. Suddenly, I was at a loss for words. I hadn't thought this far ahead. So, I said the truth.

"I wanted to say hello. I heard we'll be together for a while."

"That's one way of putting it." He said grimly, before his mouth turned up slightly, what I suspected was his version of a smile, "It's a pleasure, my lady. We look forward to leading you back to our home."

I pushed back the warmth that was welling with Eunora, *He doesn't hate me*, she cried. What a low bar.

"Thank you, Sir Rellar," I matched him with a small smile of my own, "What time are we leaving? Father didn't say."

"Not until Dreya shines down on us –it's a long journey. There's no reason to suffer on the first day."

I nodded, peeking around Sir Rellar. I scanned the other knights –all of whom had straightened up and paused what they were doing to watch the exchange. Twenty-two eyes fixed on me. My stomach turned. *Too many eyes. Too much attention.*

"I–" My voice caught, and I frowned and looked back to Sir Rellar. Shaking my head, I said, "I won't bother you anymore. I'll be ready tomorrow. Thank you."

"Of course, my lady." His face was not kind, he was too grizzled for that, but his voice was kind enough. That was a nice change from the usual cold, judgemental tone of the Dawns.

Nodding, I raised my hand and waved at the other knights before turning around and all but bolting out of the training grounds.

My stomach was turning, and as soon as I turned the corner, I began running back to the hedge maze –my bag hitting my side with the force of my movement. I wasn't as fast as Sir Rellar, I didn't move like a lightning bolt, but I was *fast*. What had been a several minute long trek turned to mere seconds, and it was *just* fast enough as I rounded one of the corners in the maze. I came to a halt, dropped Noir, and bent over.

I threw up, propping myself up unsteadily against a hedge. Eunora's anxiety was too much. And as I spit out bile, I grit my teeth.

"This is ridiculous," I hissed. And then I threw up again.

It was several minutes before my body had settled, and I felt confident enough to pick up Noir and make my way back to my room. Fortunately, I'd brought a bag and had more than enough mana for [Weave of Darkness]. Climbing up through the window was child's play.

I nearly scrubbed my skin raw as I washed off the vomit. My nails scratched at my skin, and I was simmering with irritation.

That fear was not my own.

It was not of my world.

It was a fear from here, from a body that was slowly becoming my own –but was not yet truly mine.

"[Shadow Conjuration] [Shadow Manipulation]"

I let the darkness spill from me, filling the near-empty bathroom. It spread from me like a fog, darkening all that it touched. The coldness of shadow against skin gave me comfort –even if it did not soothe the anger boiling beneath my veins. Even if it did not calm the irritation that was born from being Eunora. All it did was put on a stopper on it, kicking the can down the road.

And it made me want my name. I craved it.

Say your name. Say it. Find it within you, it has to be there. I made a wish to the universe.

"My name is –!" My voice caught as a spike of pain shot through my head.

[System Notice: The skill [Tight Lips] has been forcefully activated. Strike Cause: User attempt to

utter Otherworldly name. Data currently purged. Strike Null.]

I grit my teeth. I needed something from *elsewhere*. Anything. I had been shoving my memories down because every thought caused me pain. Caused me anger. But now I needed it. I needed a name.

"*Emmett.*" I whispered it so gently, so softly I was sure even the Gods wouldn't be able to hear me, "I miss you."

I was wrong.

I screamed in shock as another, stronger pain went through me. It felt as if every nerve in my body was lit aflame.

[System Notice: The skill [Tight Lips] has been forcefully activated for the first time. Strike Cause: User uttered Otherworldly information in the perception of another. Strike recorded.]

That caused my heart to leap. *In the perception of another.* I felt my body begin to shake as I looked around the shadow-filled bathroom.

"Who's there?" My voice shook, but really that was the least of my worries.

Silence answered me.

I cut off my Skills, letting the bathroom settle into the dull grey of natural darkness. Still, I could see no one.

"Hello?"

I jumped as a knock resounded on the door, "My Lady? Are you all right?"

The voice was familiar, and I snapped my eyes to the door. *Maria.* I hadn't heard her in my room, but that made little sense. She was a maid. I should be able to pick up on her presence. *Right? Isn't that the point of having a [Rare] Class?* I felt another shiver run through me at the thought of another weakness, another ignorance.

"I–" My voice caught, and I cleared my throat, "Is anyone else with you?"

"No, my Lady, it's just me. I've come with snacks, so you will have something to do while I move the boxes from your room."

"All right, I'll be out shortly."

Slowly, I rose from the bath, trying not to let the fear running through me continue to control me. I shook as I began drying off and then dressing. I took deep breaths as I combed and braided my hair. It was a while before I was calm enough to leave the bathroom.

As I walked out, my blue eyes met Maria's golden ones, and she gave a curtsy, "Would you like some tea?"

I nodded and went to the last plush chair in my room and the small end table next to it. They were all that was left besides my bed and two outfits hanging in my closet –one to sleep in and one to travel in. Next to the chair was a shining cart that had a teapot and a tower of treats.

As I sat, Maria handed me a book.

Divine Tales of the Illustrious Gods by Illera Mrovin.

"I found this tucked away in your closet," Maria spoke softly as if she was calming a wild animal. Maybe she was, "Should I pack it?"

I swallowed. This was the book Eunora had traded all that extra work for. Lina had given it to her just before I awoke. The one with the deeper stories.

186

"No, I'll keep it with me."

Eunora had yet to read it. But this felt like something I could do to bring her peace. To bring *me* peace. So, as Maria made her trips back and forth, I read the book. I took in every gruesome detail, every mystical power, every heroic deed, every villain taken to task. That was how I spent my last night in this wretched estate. Doing something for Eunora.

I fell asleep curled up with the book, and when I awoke in the morning, I gently tucked the book in with Noir and Haze into my bag.

It was a slow morning, and I didn't notice much. No one came to see me off –not the Countess or the Count, not Evelyn or Raphael. Not Theodore. Not the twins. And I was glad for it. If I could never see their faces again, it would be too soon.

That was how I left the Dawn estate.

Without pomp or ceremony. As if I was a ghost disappearing into the miasma. Or a shadow overcome by the sun.

Epilogue One

Maeve, A Field Guide

By Cellum Biome, Lunar Year 1251, Solar Year 626

Preface, Page 2

The Queendom of Maeve: Long has it been a central power on the continent of Opalle. Maeve takes up a quarter of the continent and is bordered by sovereign nations on the Northern, Southern, and Western sides – with the Eastern side facing the Quiet Ocean.

Interesting Facts about the Queendom: Maeve is both feared and resented by its neighbors –unless you look to a small country on its southern border named Gracek. But no one looks to that nation, not even Maeve. The mountains that surround the Queendom tower into the domain of dragons, so aerial transport is unable to cross most of the borderlands. Thus, their only entry points are sporadic valleys between mountain ranges. Very few valleys are low enough for a flight path to be viable, despite the several gaps in the border mountains.

Chapter One: On The Basic Structure of Life in Maeve, Page 15, 19, 25

Sights to see: …One such gap that, while present, is still higher elevation than possible to fly through is the valley at the border town of Fellan. On the Western edge of Maeve, it is densely forested and nestled between the Galation and Skylar mountain ranges. It connects the Callistan Empire to the Queendom. This has often been one of the stronger borders between Maeve and their neighbors.

Organizations of Note: Overseen by one of the Ducal families of Maeve, Fellan is home to several knighthoods, such as the Dusk and the Golden Griffiths, and a well-respected swordsmanship academy named for the city itself...

Bestiary of Maeve: ... Across the mountainous regions of Maeve, several beasts are generated by the aether, from griffins in the south to kelpies in the east. There are even records of arrakoras to the north. Central and Western Maeve are plagued most prominently by the Blight. The Blight is caused by mana corruption in dense forests. It is well known that the Blight consisted of various sub-monsters, but the most prominent is the Tree Blight. Averaging seven feet, the monstrosity is made up of the desiccated corpse of a mana tree or related flora. There are several lower-tiered variants, such as the Sap Blight, Vine Blight, and Twig Blights.

Time of the year to avoid: The Blights intensify every winter and taper off by the end of summer. Often the forest in the foothills of each mountain range must be cleared of large sources of corruption to prevent even further decay of the forests. Every Solar Year, well-traveled adventurers will clear out the sources of corruption in summer and autumn, less the corruption gather into a dungeon.

Chapter Four: On Regional Differences in the Queendom, Pages 62, 68, 74, and 82

Sights to see: ... Across Western Maeve, in the lands of the Duke and Duchess Dawn, the Ancestral Count, it is not uncommon for wolf-beasts to roam. Due to the nature of the West, most of these beasts have affinities with wind or water, but on occasion, light, fire, and earth have been noted. Please be aware, should you encounter a beast with a natural shadow affinity, it is inadvisable to fight. The spirits of shadow seldom choose humanoid races, and thus many of their tricks are unknown.

Key Place of Interest: … Oberon, the Royal City, sits within a basin surrounded by mountains. From foothill to foothill, every inch of Central Maeve makes up Oberon, and the mountains are both a danger and protector to those that dwell within Oberon. Nadine, the Capital of the East, sits upon an island surrounded by silver bridges that lead to the city proper, and from the highest tower, the Tower of Privy, the lord of the city can see the Quiet Ocean —and any possible incursions. Within the North sits the Moors of Herenel. The land is clear for the lords to see from all angles. No trees or mountains or even a hill for miles around allow the people of Nemo to live and protect themselves from the dangers of the forest. The Duke of Poplar protects his people from his home in Titania, the Capital of the South, with its artisans and adventurers spread across the many small towns of the bread basket that is the South. Adaline, the Capital of the West, is a city without walls —instead opting for the protection of barrier mages. Such mages study for years to contract with light spirits in order to gain an applicable [Class]. The Barrier Master of Adaline, Nostradamus Pine, had been so for over a hundred and fifty years and, while infamous for his temper, is well respected for his capability.

What Is the Queen's Contingent? … Outside of Juvel, Maybell, and Wig, there are few true cities in the west — instead, the land is made up of logging and mining villages and occasionally a town large enough for the Queen to deem it worth monitoring with a contingent from the Capital. These contingents are usually made up of one Administrator, one Magister, and one Sword Master. Each of them comes with their own retinue varying in size based on the population of the town they are to be dispatched to. It is the Administrator's duty to oversee the function of the town and surrounding area, collect taxes due to the crown, and handle any noble disputes in their jurisdiction. The Magister is set to oversee the magical protections of the area and to monitor magics taught at any mage schools. The Sword Master is to handle any incursions of beasts, monitor the physical protections of the town, and oversee any martial academies that set up in the area.

Key Place of Interest: … in Oberon, the Capital, the Queen sits with her court and oversees each of the four regions —the Duchy of Umbra to the East, the Duchy of Nemo to the North, the Duchy of Poplar to the South, and the Duchy of Dawn to the West. Each of the families are pillars of Maeve —Umbra brings a wealth of coastal goods, Nemo brings the most artisans and tradespeople, Poplar is the home of the populace, and Dawn is a bastion against incursions both within and without. All serve in their ancestral homes. Dawn from Adaline, Nemo from the Moors of Hernel, Poplar from Titania, and Umbra from the Tower of Privy.

Chapter Fourteen: On the Duchy of Dawn and Their Sordid History, Page 142

Quote: … It is unknown how the ancestral counts became Dukes and Duchesses due to the Travesty of Nemo several hundred years prior to this publication. However, it can be assumed it was much like how they have grown their power since —through might and bloodshed. And large broods of children…

Chapter Seventeen: On the Duchy of Nemo and The Nemoan Travesties, Page 189

Quote: ... Nemo has maintained their Ducal seat through a [Unique] [Class] that is presumably known only to the Queen and her Royal Heirs. Such a Class often results in semi-regular smiting by one or other of the Divines, and such became the centennial tradition of the Nemoan Travesties. This humble scholar has never once questioned the Queen's wisdom of allowing such a [Class] to remain in existence...

Continued in Otherworldy, Vol. 2.

If you can't stand waiting, head to Royal Road to read the most up-to-date chapters for FREE!